THE SPIDER:
DEATH'S CRIMSON JUGGERNAUT

MASTER OF MEN!

THE SPIDER®

DEATH'S CRIMSON JUGGERNAUT

By Grant Stockbridge

ALTUS PRESS • 2019

PUBLISHING HISTORY

"Death's Crimson Juggernaut" originally appeared in the November, 1934 (Vol. 4, No.
2) issue of *The Spider* magazine. Copyright 2019 by Argosy Communications, Inc.
All rights reserved.

CHAPTER 1
THE CRUCIFIX MURDERS

THE GIRL shrank back against the dresser. Her hand, clutching the throat of her kimono, was white and strained, the fingers almost tearing the flimsy black silk.

"Don't!" she pleaded. "Oh, God, don't! I've suffered enough!"

The Spider smiled thinly. Inwardly he was as tense as this lovely frightened girl, with her face pale beneath the banner of her glowing red hair. He knew that three killers were on their way even now to kidnap her—to murder her. He knew that he was only scant moments ahead of the men... If they found the Spider here, their flaming guns would make short work of them both. "The Spider never persecutes the innocent," he said slowly, emphatically, fighting the tenseness from his voice. "I am here to help you."

The girl did not appear to hear him. "First those gangsters half-crucify me," she moaned her litany of suffering. "Then the police send grandfather to the asylum for something he didn't do, and now you... *you....*"

"Stop that!" Wentworth ordered sharply.

The girl's voice was tinged with hysteria. There was terror in the wide gaze that studied the sallow, taut-skinned face of the Spider. The beaked nose which Richard Wentworth had created as part of his disguise was aggressive, but there was kindliness in the blue-gray eyes. He was planning a welcome for the kill-

ers, but before he could prepare it, he must win this girl's confidence. He wore a disguise that men everywhere recognized as the Spider, wide black hat upon lanky long hair, a swirling cloak across a hunched back. Those gangsters would know him instantly—and the underworld had reason to hate him. The frantic need of haste spurred him on.

"Listen, Caroline," he said to the girl. "Helping people everywhere is my mission, despite the false ideas you get from the newspapers. I read of your grandfather's case, and I'm here to help you."

Under the persuasion of Wentworth's pleasant voice, of his

magnetic personality, the girl's terror began to fade. Her hand dropped from the throat of her kimono. Curiosity was supplanting the fear with which she gazed at this almost legendary figure whose name flashed across the pages of newspapers only when great criminals menaced the people. He struck then, horribly, and men died with the crimson seal of the Spider upon their foreheads.

It was this that had bred her terror—for her grandfather had been accused of ghastly crimes. Police said that, in the grip of religious mania, he had crucified three persons alive and had attempted to kill his own grand-daughter the same way!

"Is it—is it possible," the girl stammered, "that you have become interested in our case?"

Her hand was half-reaching out to him now in appeal. Wentworth saw upon the upturned palm a red scar where a cruel nail had been driven through it—by her grandfather police said. The scar was not round, but a long jagged slit. After the nail had pierced her hand, her entire weight had been allowed to sag upon it....

Wentworth drew in a deep breath. He had won the girl's confidence now. He must hurry on with his plans. Those gangsters might even now be at the door!

"In a few minutes," he told the girl, "the gangsters who framed your grandfather will be here again. They are after you this time...."

The girl choked back a cry, fist pressed against her mouth.

"... But I will protect you," Wentworth continued. "If you

will help me, perhaps we can trap these men and free your grandfather."

RAPIDLY, THEN, he outlined his plans. He had been on his way to investigate the girl's case, and with his usual thoroughness, he had scouted out the neighborhood before entering the building where Caroline and her grandfather, Preston Davis, lived in furnished rooms. A luxurious sedan parked on the deserted street of the poverty-stricken district had aroused his suspicions. Creeping up behind the auto, he heard two men whispering in the car, overheard the plot to kill the girl! The two gangsters were waiting only the arrival of a third man who was due at any moment.

The Spider could easily have routed the two, or called police to arrest them, but it was never his method to do things by halves. He knew that the crimes of which the girl's grandfather was accused had some hidden motive, that there was a keen brain behind them. There would be no point in seizing these minor crooks and letting the greater criminal go, so he had hurried to the girl's rooms to prepare a trap.

Once in his power, he felt confident he could make the killers betray the hidden motive—and the master-criminal behind it.

So the Spider waited to face these three. Guns would flame in that moment. If gangster lead did not find him first, three more killers would pay for their crimes. For another man such a course undoubtedly would have meant certain suicide. But the Spider?… It was not for nothing that he was known as the Master of Men!

The Crucifixion Murders, of which Preston Davis had been

accused, all had been committed in the block of lodging-houses in which the girl's home was located. First an artist living in a fifth floor studio had been gagged, then nailed to the wall with spikes through his hands and feet. He had been allowed to dangle there until he died from shock and loss of blood. Two other identical murders had followed in rapid succession. A young sales-girl had been stripped naked and nailed up; then the landlady of a rooming house had met the same fate. And after each killing, tenants recalled that they heard cracked, half-mad laughter as though a torturing madman chortled over the suffering of his victims.

By the time the third murder had been revealed—and all were apparently without motive—terror had spread throughout the block of houses in which the crimes had been committed, and there was a general exodus of tenants. The sheer unreasoning brutality of the deaths terrified them. The climax came when screams of a girl brought police rushing to the rooms of Preston Davis to find his granddaughter—the red-headed girl who faced Wentworth now—naked against the wall, a nail through the palm of one hand while Davis himself held a bloody-headed hammer.

It was in vain the girl protested that three masked men had undressed her and nailed her to the wall. It was in vain that Davis swore to that same story. He had been hailed before a court and adjudged insane. The murders had ceased and the public were satisfied. But the girl kept up her battle to free her grandfather. She told court after court about those three masked men. That, Wentworth suspected, was why the gangsters were coming back. Caroline was talking too much and ultimately someone might believe her story as even the Spider did.

Wentworth concluded his instructions for trapping the three men, and the girl nodded breathlessly, brown eyes sliding toward the door which at any moment might resound to the knock of the killers.

"I understand," she said softly, "but you're sure...."

"They won't try to kill you here," Wentworth said emphatically. "That would prove to police that the story you've been telling in the courts was true. They want to make it seem that you have given up the fight and left the city..." He stopped in mid-sentence as an unwary foot creaked on a board in the hall. He nodded to the girl, reached the window in a stride. For an instant he poised on the sill, then vanished into the night. He seemed to have stepped into the air. Actually, he had put a foot into a loop of powerfully-made silk rope, a line a little smaller than a lead pencil which nevertheless could lift seven-hundred pounds. The line was fastened about a chimney on the roof and by this means he had descended.

SCARCELY HAD he disappeared when an imperative knock shook the girl's door. "Open up, Miss Davis," a man said gruffly. "We're from the police."

"What do you want?" the girl demanded sharply. Wentworth, peering in, could just glimpse the sheen of her kimono molded to the tense lines of her body as she crouched against the door.

Wentworth could not make out the deep-voiced response from the other side of the door, but he heard the bolt click, saw the girl reel backward before the charge of three masked men.

Her cry was instantly muffled by a hand slapped cruelly across her lips.

"Keep quiet," the leader snarled, still crushing the girl's mouth with his palm. "You won't get hurt, see? Joe, pull down that shade."

A second man strode to the window, snapped down the ancient curtain. It was prickled with light holes. Wentworth smiled thinly. They were making it easier for him. He put a foot soundlessly on the sill, crouched there to listen. He had assured the girl she would be safe from harm while she was in her home. Logically, she would be, but he must make sure. If they moved to kill Caroline Davis, the Spider's deadly guns would go into action, one man against three. He listened tensely, peering through a small crack in the shade.

"We ain't going to hurt you," the man said once more, his voice harsh. "If you promise not to squawl, you don't even have to be gagged."

The girl must have assented, although Wentworth could not see, for the man who had been throttling her stepped back, and she began to talk. "What have you come back for?" she demanded bitterly. "The police don't want you. Nobody will listen to me."

"You're talking too much," the leader said bluntly. "We're shipping you out of town."

"I won't go," Caroline said stubbornly. "I know what's behind this business, and I know who has hired you to do this. I'm going…" She cried out suddenly, and Wentworth's muscles tensed at the sound of a fist striking soft white flesh. It made blood throb hotly in his temples, but he remained quiet. This had to be.

"I said you talked too much," the leader growled. "You spill what you know right here and now, or you ain't going away… Not anywhere you want to go. Get the idea, girl friend?"

Wentworth sought another peephole. Ah, he could see the girl now. The leader had slammed her against the wall and a thread of blood distorted her mouth. She stood with hands clenched at her sides, red head held high. Her eyes were scornful.

"You talk," the leader ground out, "or else…" He ripped the kimono from her shoulder and his fingers bit into the white flesh. Wentworth saw Caroline's teeth close on her lower lip.

"Joe," the leader said, "suppose you work on her arms."

Sweat broke out on Wentworth's forehead as the girl's shoulders knotted with the man's twisting. She sagged forward, dropped to her knees. "I won't! I won't!" she gasped.

Actually, she couldn't. She was doing as Wentworth had instructed and the knowledge that it was his doing, the moans of the suffering girl, ate like hot iron into his vitals. He clenched his fists to hold himself in check. He must wait, must endure this in the hope that, under stress, one of these men might blurt out a betraying phrase—something that might lead him to the master-brain behind these murderous activities.

"Oh, please, please!" the girl sobbed. "Help me! I can't… can't…."

WENTWORTH'S LIPS twisted. He was a humane man, one who loved his fellows, else he would never have dedicated himself as the Spider to the service of mankind. He had expected this and had warned the girl what might come. Nevertheless, it was hard to cling to an abstract ideal of service when torturers were working upon weak flesh. Yet if the girl gave way, if she confessed to these killers that her claim to definite knowledge was a lie, all her suffering would have been in vain. And she was weakening. That last cry for help showed that.

Wentworth drew his weapon, a powerful, nearly silent air-pistol. If the girl kept quiet an instant longer, he still might triumph. His trick had failed, but it might be possible to turn the tables on these men, to force them to talk as they had sought to torture information from Caroline Davis.

Despite the fact that there were three men in the room, three men with ready guns that would blast bloody death at the Spider, there was no hesitancy in Wentworth's actions.

With a tight smile upon his lips, the Spider sprang into the room of torture!

The Spider who had talked with Caroline Davis had been a pleasant, smiling man. Though she had never seen him before, had only read his name with a shudder of dread, she had trusted him after looking into his gray-blue eyes.

The Spider who leaped into the room now was smiling also, but his lips were stiff with anger, and his smile was a fearful thing. His eyes were flame. He announced his presence with the *ping* of his air pistol.

The man called Joe relaxed his hold on the girl's tortured arms. He jerked erect with wild, surprised eyes, but even as he straightened, his eyes lost all expression; his body went lax and he pitched sideways to the floor. Wentworth's tiny bullet had crashed through his forehead and torn the life from his brain.

"Up with them," snapped Wentworth. "Sky high!"

The two other men whirled as if the same muscles moved both. One held his gun ready and once more Wentworth's curiously-shaped weapon released death with a small *ping* of discharged air. As before, the pellet struck the man between the eyes. The weight of his automatic seemed to pull him downward. His whole body followed it to the floor.

The remaining man, the leader, lifted his hands and let his gun fall with a dull clatter. The whites of his eyes showed entirely around the pale irises. His mouth opened and closed, but no sound came from it. Wentworth eyed him, still with that twisted tight smile upon his lips. He, too, was silent, but that deadly pistol was leveled on the gangster's forehead.

The girl still crouched where the torturers had left her, doubled forward upon silken knees, the kimono nearly torn from her body. She lifted her head, and her brown, suffering eyes fixed not upon the gangsters but upon Wentworth's face. She seemed unconscious of the slain men, of the terror in the one who remained alive.

Wentworth broke the silence: "I see that you know me," he said softly to the gangster chief. "Let that make you careful in your answers. *Who is your master?*"

The dead-white pallor of the man's face increased. His straw-colored hair, bristling out from under a low-crowned derby, seemed dark by comparison. He did not speak.

"Speak, fool!" snapped Wentworth. "The Spider asks you a question!"

Even the dread name of the Master of Men did not loosen the man's tongue. His head began to shake from side to side slowly, as if some power outside himself were turning it. Wentworth took a slow stride toward him, the air-pistol rising.

"I can't!" the man stammered, his voice high with strain. "I can't tell! I don't know!"

WENTWORTH SAW that the man was absolutely terrified. No threat of death could frighten him more, could drag another word from him. He was more afraid of his master than of the Spider! Wentworth recognized that fact with a narrowing of his eyes.

The man winced before the gaze of this hunchbacked man in a cloak. Involuntary tremors ran through his body. He knew that the Spider killed without mercy when it would advance the ends of justice—that he executed criminals as coldly, as surely, as the State's electric chair. Yet knowing these things, he did not obey the Spider's orders. Truly, his master must be a fearful man!

However, if the man could not be forced to talk, there still were ways of learning his secrets. He could be allowed to escape and then be followed.

Wentworth made his muscles jerk in a start of false surprise, spun toward the open window as if he had caught a suspicious noise there. He took a full stride toward it before the terrified gang-leader could gather his dazed senses and take advantage of his opportunity. The creak of a floor board betrayed his first move. Caroline Davis screamed and Wentworth threw himself to the floor. He rolled and loosed a deliberately wide shot which burned past the man's face. The gangster darted for the door.

Wentworth could have shot the man three times while he fumbled with the knob, jerked open the door and plunged into the hall, but he only watched with a queer smile. When the man had gone, he turned to Caroline. She had scrambled to her feet and was dragging the remnants of her kimono about her.

"You are a brave woman," Wentworth told her simply, and once more his eyes were pleasant. "Take this money and register at the Martha Washington Hotel as Frances Richards. I'll look you up there. Together we'll set your grandfather free."

He smothered the girl's protests. For a man who intended trailing a murderer to the den of his master, he seemed strangely unhurried. Yet he made not a single unnecessary movement. He stooped between the two dead men, and on the forehead of each he pressed the base of a small platinum cigarette-lighter. When he pocketed the gadget again, a crimson spot gleamed on each corpse's forehead, a spot which had sprawling hairy legs and fearsome fangs—*the seal of the Spider!*

Before the girl's gasp had died, Wentworth was at the window, and had drawn in his silken line. Less than thirty seconds after the gang leader left the room, the Spider was ready to go, too.

"Get out immediately," he told the girl. "And don't worry about those bodies. The police will know whom to blame."

With a brief smile, he was gone, striding long-legged along the hall. He dropped downstairs with deceptively slow movements that nevertheless covered the distance with great rapidity. His approach of each floor was cautious, his keen eyes alert for ambush. But he reached the street without meeting a foe and shambled along, an ungainly hunchbacked figure in a black cloak and slouch hat. He turned to the right and skirted shadows.

There was a movement within them and a swarthy man bowed with cupped hands to his forehead, a Hindu *salaam*.

"The evil one fled in a Ford coupé, *sahib*," the man said in swift, distinct English. "He turned right. The license number...."

"It is well, Ram Singh," Wentworth nodded to his faithful Hindu servant and bodyguard. "Follow me. Usual instructions."

The hunched figure of the Spider reached the curb in two long strides, sprang into a powerful, long-hooded roadster and instantly was purring down the street. He took the right turn, blazed along for two blocks, and slowed—a half block behind a Ford coupé with a license number he recognized. He touched the horn twice, then went past with a deeper muttering of his motor. A man raised his hand in salute in the other car. Wentworth had taken over the trail from Jackson, his chauffeur extraordinary, who had served under him as sergeant during the World War.

AHEAD OF him, the Spider saw the fleeing car of the gang-

RICHARD
WENTWORTH

ster. It was darting like a frightened chicken through the traffic
of late evening. The night was mild with the infrequent warmth
that drops upon New York sometimes in early November and
scores of automobiles thronged the streets. The fugitive caught a
green light and whirled left. Wentworth made the turn and was
not a hundred feet behind when the Ford swung right beneath

the long-legged stilts of the elevated railroad along Columbus Avenue.

Without warning, the Ford swerved to the curb. Before it had braked to a halt, the gangster was out, pelting hard-heeled toward a narrow entrance between garish shop fronts. He did not once look behind him. Wentworth parked, strode rapidly toward the doorway. In his right hand he now grasped a heavy automatic. That air-pistol was good for close-up work in good light. In the darkness, he preferred the impact of forty-five caliber lead.

An elevated train made distant rumbling thunder and clattered nearer sluggishly. A boy and girl sat together on a stone stoop before an apartment doorway. They were laughing with a secrecy that cut them off from all the passing world. Yet within yards of them had passed a man guilty of torture and murder— and on his trail strode that most fearsome of all of humanity's grim avengers, the Spider.

On the verge of plunging into the unlighted doorway where the other had entered, Wentworth paused. There was need of speed if he were to run to earth the fiendish master of the killers. Yet the Spider was loath to crash into underworld darkness unless he spied out the surroundings. This once, though, he must chance it.

With tightening lips, Wentworth slipped into the dark doorway. He listened intently, but the thrashing of the elevated train drowned all other sound. He waited until it slammed past before he pushed on. Cautious-footed, keen-eared, he eased up stairs that showed no light.

Suddenly Wentworth froze into immobility, then he sprang frantically up the steps. Two things that spoke of death for the Spider had happened at the same instant. Behind him, he heard a slither of steel, then a clang that chopped off all sound from the street. Despite its unexpectedness, he knew what that meant. A steel portcullis, a sliding door, had dropped behind him and cut off retreat!

The other sound was laughter, cracked, eerie laughter that pimpled Wentworth's back with gooseflesh, that made cold prickles of apprehension ripple across his scalp. He knew instantly that it was the same mad mirth that had marked the crucifixion murders. He knew that it sounded now to herald his own death. He was in a trap of the killers!

As he leaped up the stairs, charging the men he knew waited to pour powder-heated lead down upon him, Wentworth's gun blazed. He ripped bullets toward the spot where that laughter had sounded. The response was not the deadly hail he had expected. In the narrow hallway that still trembled with the echoes of his shot, there was a sharp detonation like the explosion of a bursting electric light bulb. No need to see grayish vapor rising like a ghost in the darkness. Wentworth recognized the sound of a gas-bomb bursting. He felt the instantaneous smarting of his eyes.

Good God! Weren't the odds enough in the gangsters' favor already? The Spider was trapped against a steel door in a narrow slot where even a paralytic could not fail to find him with deadly lead. And now—*he was being blinded with tear gas!*

CHAPTER 2
"I SURRENDER!"

STILL RACING up the stairs, Wentworth made strangling, sneezing sounds as if the gas were torturing the membranes of his throat and nose. He snatched off his hat, crushed it tightly over his face and stumbled on blindly. They would believe him helpless, he hoped, and would not bother to use guns in the darkness.

Grim thoughts were racing through Wentworth's mind. He could not believe that ordinary killers took these precautions. He knew that the trap had not been rigged deliberately for him because only three men had known of his intervention in the case. Two of those were dead and the third had entered this building only seconds ahead of him without having had a chance to flash a warning ahead.

The fact that the gangsters were ready with a carefully planned trap, with this steel portcullis rigged and gas bombs waiting, showed careful thought and perfect organization. He had reached out to protect a young girl—and found himself in a murder trap!

The steps ended beneath Wentworth's feet and he reeled on, uncovering his face and finding that he had fought clear of the gas. His eyes smarted and streamed with tears; they were swollen nearly shut, but he had escaped the full effects of the fumes. At least he could see. If hostile eyes watched him in the unlighted hall, they saw a groping, blinded man who felt his way along the walls.

Slowly, he fumbled the full length of the hall, found no exits. There was no window at its far end, and coming back along the other side, he discovered no doors, either. He was sealed in a narrow corridor, at the mercy of fiends who killed by torture! The cracked laughter rang out again.

Wentworth's muscles jerked taut, but he fought down his panic. There must be some further plans for him, Wentworth reasoned, than merely shooting him down in this hallway. Why else would the tear gas have been used? Through the paroxysms of coughing which he still assumed at widening intervals, Wentworth gasped out words.

"I surrender!" he cried. "Don't shoot! I surrender!" He flung his automatic noisily to the floor.

Instantly blinding light flashed on from the ceiling. Wentworth stood to his full hunch-backed height, his cheeks wet with the tears that streamed from his eyes. He did not cringe nor whine for mercy. He must not overdo his "surrender," else these men would become suspicious. They all knew the fearlessness of the Spider.

Absolute silence lay upon the hallway in its bath of blazing white light. Wentworth knew that hostile eyes were studying him and he let his hands hang limply at his sides while his inflamed eyes peered straight ahead blindly. His automatic glinted on the floor.

"Throw down also that air-pistol of yours," a cold voice ordered.

There was nothing to indicate the origin of the voice. In that narrow hall, it echoed flatly. But there was no mistaking the hatred in its gloating accents. Wentworth made a pretense of resistance.

"I haven't got it any more," he protested. "I lost it while I was chasing that killer of yours."

Wentworth's hat jerked upon his head, and the hall was filled with the crashing thunder of a pistol shot. When the reverberations had died, the cold voice spoke again: "That was a warning, the next shot...."

Hurriedly Wentworth snatched the air pistol from his pocket and tossed that also to the floor. His stalling had accomplished two things. He had convinced them that he was really helpless, and he had located at least one of the men. Six feet down the hall, his bleary eyes had spotted the flaming muzzle of the gun that had fired on him through a masked loophole. He had not flinched at that shot piercing his hat; his head had not turned toward the gun, but beneath the relaxed surrender of his poise, he was alertly ready.

BEFORE HIS swollen eyes, doors began to open in the walls. Sheets of steel rose into the ceiling from before ordinary doorways and men stepped out with ready guns. The man directly before him held a Thompson sub-machine gun with its snout leveled at the Spider's body. If he squeezed that trigger, forty-five caliber bullets would cut him in half like tearing knives. The gunman was the gangster with the straw-colored hair and the pale face whom Wentworth had followed to this trap.

Wentworth did not challenge the man to action. He stood

motionless while swift hands found and removed his last gun beneath his right armpit.

The machine gunner's face was scowling: "Now shall I give it to him, chief?" he demanded.

"You'll do what you're told," came the coldly hostile voice again. "Walk straight ahead, Spider. I want to have a little talk with you."

Blindly, ignoring the machine gun that gaped before him, Wentworth stalked forward. The pale-faced gangster stood motionless for a moment, wavering between his hatred of the man who had killed his companions and his fear of the man, still unseen, who had ordered him to wait. Finally fear of the latter prevailed, but Wentworth was then so close that the man was forced to skip hurriedly aside.

As he leaped, his shoulder brushed the door jamb behind him and he stumbled off balance. It was the break for which Wentworth had been playing. Swift as a bullet, he sprang upon the man. He did not strike, nor snatch at the gun, but seized the gangster by the shoulder and spun his body before him as a shield. From behind, the long arms of the Spider reached forward, seized the machine gun.

Automatics bellowed in the close hall.

"Shoot through Mike," the cold voice ordered calmly. "He deserves to die for that fool play."

Mike screamed piercingly and the cry ended in a strangling cough as bullets plunked into his body. Wentworth held him erect, braced against the punch of heavy lead. Deliberately he swept the length of the hall with a stream of machine gun lead.

21

Over his head he caught the faint whisper of the steel door dropping. He dodged backward, thrust the body of the gangster into the path of the door. The portcullis slid down before his face, struck across the sagging neck of the gangster, Mike. Wentworth snatched the machine gun clear, whirled toward the room behind him. It was empty, but there might be loopholes in its walls.

He was not locked in because his swift action had jammed the portcullis with Mike's body. If the need arose now he could retreat, but that was not his immediate plan. He crouched in the doorway and his eyes searched the room minutely. Finally he found what he sought, a round black aperture in the sidewall, a loop-hole.

Instantly, Wentworth's machine gun belched again and white plaster dust flew. The small hole became a large one and a man's muffled death cry rang. In that moment the lights blinked out. A leap carried the Spider half across the room on soundless feet. In another second, he reached the break his bullets had carved

22

NITA VAN SLOAN

in the wall. He thrust the muzzle through. With swift fingers he knotted a noose of silken cord about the trigger. As the deadly hail blazed out, he spun back to the steel door which the gangster's dead body propped open. It was the work of an instant to wriggle through the narrow slit. The machine gun chattered on.

Soft-footed, the Spider found his own weapons again, guns whose balance was so familiar that he could speed their lead unerringly in the darkness with more facility than an ordinary man might point his finger. Upon his lips, that tight small smile that was his fighting grin played again. He could escape now, but only when he could serve justice best by flight did the Spider retreat from the battle—and this time he felt that justice demanded the death of these men in their own trap.

THE SPIDER stayed. Intense silence brooded over the building. Wentworth knew it must have been carefully soundproofed, for not a sound penetrated from out of doors. But the silence was deeper than that. The building had the feeling of a deserted house. With his recognition of that fact, the Spider realized another thing. If the gang failed to destroy him, they must know that this headquarters was of no further value to them, despite all its careful preparation.

One instant, Wentworth was standing with guns ready to battle the entire gang. The next, he had flung himself down on his belly and was wriggling again beneath the steel doorway. He leaped across the room, found the fastenings of iron shutters and flung them wide. Seconds later he was gliding down the face of the building on the silken cord that the police called his web. He did not pause to draw it after him, but flung himself frantically from the alley.

"When rats leave a ship, wise men stay ashore," says an ancient adage. Wentworth had realized that the building was deserted. A sudden hunch made him flee, too. As he burst from the alley, he whirled abruptly to the left. Guns blazed across the narrow street, from dark doorways and windows, the reports drowned in the clatter of a passing elevated train. But the Spider was a hunched shadow among shadows. Lead chipped the walk at his feet, smacked against the brick wall, but did not hit him. Then… behind him, all hell cut loose.

With a bellowing detonation, the entire building he had just quitted lifted toward the sky as if on tiptoes, then fell in upon itself. The gust of the concussion hurled Wentworth flat, swept a howling hurricane up the street. Even through the blast, he caught the piercing wail of the elevated train's whistle. He twisted about and stared upward. The explosion had torn a great gap in the tracks. Screams and shrieks rose shrilly… The train, with grinding brakes, slid into the gap, crashed with a ripping shattering of its wooden cars into the street!

It seemed foolishly like some child's toy, car after car being dragged nose-down through the sagging gap in the tracks. Men and women leaped from the car windows. Others were dragged screaming to death in the splintered wreckage below. A great green-white flare of electric flame leaped from the third rail and within seconds, fire was licking the ruins. The rattling debris of the blast pelted like shrapnel. Men and women were racing into the streets now. Fire and police sirens, the hoarser wail of ambulances, filled the air.

With a cursing sob in his throat, Wentworth whirled toward the wreckage then checked himself. Within seconds, the emergency-crew and hordes of police would be on the job. For hours they would throng the district. And while they worked over the territory, the Spider could do nothing. He stood rigidly, hands clenched at his sides.

These fiendishly callous killers had slaughtered a score or

more of human beings in an attempt to catch him. That charge must have been planted long before its use, and the havoc it would create had been calculated. Probably it had been intended to block pursuit if ever the killers were driven into flight. But the thing that ate into Wentworth's mind like acid was the utter disregard of human life and property that this gang had evidenced.

In heaven's name, what hellish brain was behind these men? What awful crimes did they plot? Men who would thus slaughter the innocents with so little need would stop at nothing to gain their ends!

But Wentworth could accomplish nothing here now while police thronged the neighborhood. Better to flee—to take up the trail again from another clue. Grimly, the Spider forced himself to turn away while the screams and moans of the dying echoed in the streets, while the blast of the sirens shrieked to a halt and the pounding feet of police raced to the scene of the disaster. He sprang to his car, backed it over humped up debris and whirled among the elevated pillars.

A policeman's whistle shrilled, but Wentworth ground the accelerator to the floor and darted on. A bullet sang past his head, then he slithered around a corner and was gone. Moments later, he rolled into the winding drives of Central Park and turned southward.

A fury of anger burned within him and his lips were pursed in a cold smile. He would wreak vengeance a thousand-fold for that senseless, murdering blast, for the innocent lives that had been wiped out there and in the crucifixion kills.

AS HE raced along, Wentworth swiftly stripped off his disguise with his free hand. The beaked nose and the lank hair disappeared. He swirled into a darkened parking area and when he swung out a few moments later, cold cream had removed the sallow, taut skin and left the lean, tanned face of Richard Wentworth. More slowly now, he drove on toward his apartment house on lower Fifth Avenue. Cloak and black hat were stowed away in secret compartments in the car and the man who alighted before the door, nodding carelessly to the *chasseur*, was a polished, suave man of the world. He looked now what he actually was, a wealthy young clubman, scion of inherited wealth, sportsman, *dilettante* of the arts.

He was handsome in a lean-cheeked, strong-jawed way and there was a hint of mockery in his smooth, arched brows. In the poise of his head there was self-reliance, even a hint of arrogance, and his square, erect shoulders showed no trace of the hunch of the Spider. One thing marred his appearance. He had forgotten, apparently, to remove smoked glasses which he sometimes wore at night to kill the glare of passing headlights. Through them, it was impossible for the attendants to see the painfully inflamed membranes of his tear-gassed eyes.

Wentworth went directly to his penthouse apartment in a private elevator. White-haired old Jenkyns, his butler, opened the door with a bow, his wrinkled face wreathed in smiles. He straightened, and, seeing the smoked glasses, allowed a shadow of alarm to cross his face.

"What is it, Master Dick?" he asked swiftly. The opening of the elevator door jerked Wentworth about in a crouch. Ram

27

Singh and Jackson, he knew, would not be coming up yet. It was their task to make sure that no one had followed him before they reported to the apartment. Then who would be coming at this time of night on his private elevator? There was only one answer. Someone had slipped past the vigilance of Ram Singh and Jackson.

But this reasoning did not take place in Wentworth's conscious mind. It was a flash of thought in his subconscious, the sort of thing that people call intuition. It whirled him about with his hand racing toward his gun.

In the doorway of the elevator two men stood.

One held a machine gun, the other gripped a hand grenade. The pin had already been yanked loose and as Wentworth turned to face the two, the man's hand was swinging forward to hurl the bomb directly at the Spider!

As he stared in the face of double death it flashed through Wentworth's brain that never before had he fought so powerful and ruthless an enemy. He had barely crossed swords with the man, had just discovered that some shrewd brain was behind the murders he investigated, and already the enemy had penetrated his identity. The Master Killer was a genius of crime. This was the second attempt to murder him within an hour—and this time there seemed no escape.

Bomb and machine gun threatened instantaneous and horrible death. But Wentworth was acting even as he thought. His automatic spat as it snapped from the clip holster and the machine gunner sagged against the rear of the elevator cage.

But the time needed for Wentworth's single shot had given

the bomber his opportunity. He tossed the grenade and it bounded with a metallic ring on the floor at Wentworth's feet.

Quick as thought, the bomber leaped backward, snatching at the elevator door. Wentworth stooped, allowing his automatic to fall to the floor. He caught up the bomb and with the same movement of his arm tossed it toward the cage. The door was already closing. The gangster's hand was on the lever, but safety devices prevented the elevator from descending until the door closed.

The grenade and the slamming door raced. The solid steel portal, faced in bronze, had two feet to slide. The grenade must travel five feet and Wentworth's throw had been no overhand heave, but a weak underhand toss. The bomb turned over slowly in the air. It seemed scarcely to move.

Wentworth spilled to his knees, off balance from his quick throw. His hands hit the floor and he lifted his head and stared. He had done his utmost, the rest depended on that door and the tumbling grenade. He saw the gangster's white, terrified face in the narrowing crack, saw that he was straining every nerve and muscle to shut the door more rapidly. Suddenly the man jerked his hand from the door. He stabbed with open palm at the slow-moving grenade, screamed in mad terror. Then the tableau vanished, cut off by the sullen clang as the door of steel and bronze clapped shut. For an instant Wentworth stared at the ornately chased door, then he hurled himself to the right and flat upon his face.

"Shut the door, Jenkyns," he shouted.

The gangster's last desperate thrust to turn the bomb had

failed. The door had closed—the instant after the grenade had flashed through the opening and into the cage. But TNT is a terrific explosive, even behind a heavy barrier of metal....

THE BLAST was fearful. It blew out Wentworth's senses like a candle in a gale. The bronze door leaped in its frame and wrenched loose, hung by one wrecked pulley. The entire top of the building went dark and the roof of the elevator shaft soared into the air and smashed into University Place, half a block away. And inside the cage....

A case-hardened interne got there first. He looked into the elevator once, then reeled weakly over to a wall and leaned there, retching.

A half hour later, Wentworth regained consciousness under the careful ministrations of his own physician whom Jenkyns had hurriedly summoned. Half-dazed, he was still able to grin whitely up into the serious face of Stanley Kirkpatrick, Commissioner of Police. Other uniformed men were in the room also.

"In the army," Wentworth said, "we always counted three before we threw a grenade. I guess that guy didn't go to France."

"Who were they?" Kirkpatrick asked harshly, his usually precise voice roughened by concern.

Wentworth rolled his head on the pillow in negative. "You might try fingerprints."

Kirkpatrick swore once raspingly. "Yes—if we can find a finger. I doubt if the bomb left that much of them in one piece. Dick, you have more luck than any other five men deserve to have." He stared intently down at him. "What's the matter with your eyes?"

Wentworth forced himself up from the couch, waving the doctor's protest aside impatiently. His head was spinning dizzily but after a few moments the room stopped dancing about.

"Some friends called on me twice tonight," he muttered, drawing a hand heavily across his forehead. "The first time they tried gas and guns; the second time, a bomb. Kirk, I want to talk to you…" He glanced about the room at the several men in uniform. The doctor was present, too, and a man in civilian clothing who had a pallid, intent face… "alone," Wentworth added.

Kirkpatrick waved his hand in dismissal and the uniformed cops faded out. Only the pale-faced man remained and Wentworth looked at him impatiently.

"Would you excuse me, please?" he asked. "I wish to talk with the Commissioner."

"I will not," the man said and his sharp jaw snapped up with a click of teeth. "If you have anything to communicate, the District Attorney's office has an interest in it, too."

Wentworth glanced quickly again at the man, studying him. He was about Wentworth's height, perhaps thirty years old, with a bleached skin that contrasted strangely with jet black hair. He was terribly thin, but there was no weakness in the set of his sharp jaw, nor in the glare of his vivid blue eyes.

"You're a stranger to me," Wentworth said slowly, "and I have nothing as yet to confide to the District Attorney's office. When I do…."

"You'll talk now, or I'll call you before the Grand Jury," the man said. Once more there was the decisive click of his teeth.

31

"Do that," said Wentworth affably. "I've always wanted to see how a Grand Jury works," He stood abruptly. "Now get out, or I'll throw you out!"

THE WEAKNESS had evaporated from him and his quiet manner carried more authority than any threatening gesture. The white-faced man recognized that fact, strode from the room without another word. The door closed gently behind him.

"I'd like it better if he'd slammed that door," Wentworth said, staring speculatively at the closed portal. "Men who control their emotions are dangerous."

"Name's Howard Boise," Kirkpatrick said slowly.

"He's been attached to me to leech in on any investigations I make."

Wentworth grimaced, then thrust Boise from his mind and told Kirkpatrick that he suspected some hidden motive behind the crucifix murders.

"I think the man behind the killings wanted to terrify that district," Wentworth concluded.

Kirkpatrick stood frowning down at the floor.

Absently he lifted a hand to his saturnine face, touched his waxed mustaches with a stroking thumb and forefinger. Despite the fact that the call to Wentworth's home had come at four o'clock in the morning, the Commissioner had come impeccably groomed, even with a gardenia in his lapel.

The Commissioner of New York's police was like that, methodical and swift. He had an intuitive gift of reasoning, too, that nearly matched Wentworth's own. They had dueled many times as Commissioner and Spider and finally Kirkpatrick had become convinced that Wentworth was the Spider—convinced, but without proof. There was an armed truce between the two men. When possible, they co-operated, for the Spider had rid the city of criminals whom Kirkpatrick could not legally touch. Yet if ever the proof fell into Kirkpatrick's hands....

He looked up abruptly, "The Spider killed two men in Caroline Davis' rooms tonight," he said, "and the girl vanished. The two men were gangsters. It looks..." a faint smile stirred Kirkpatrick's mustaches, "as if the Spider believes the same as you do—that something besides madness is behind the crucifixions. What is the motive that you suspect?"

Wentworth's lips were faintly smiling, too, but his face was completely innocent as he answered.

"I don't know why the Spider has been dragged into this conversation," he said, "but I'm glad to know the fellow subscribes to my line of thought." He waved a hand deprecatingly. "I haven't yet struck on the motive, but there are usually only two motives for terrorization. Either the terrorizer wants people to stay away from a given locality, or he wants people to leave that district. In this case, it must be the latter. As for the reason...."

Kirkpatrick abruptly smacked a fist into the palm of his hand. "I knew I'd read something that tied up with your theory," he said. "Those buildings are on a site that a certain corporation wants for a skyscraper." He paused and shook his head. "That's fantastic, though. Business men wouldn't murder for such trivial reasons."

"Trivial?" Wentworth drawled. "If I know my real estate, I'd say ten million would be a fair price for the land. Now, if it could be had for five million because of a few murders…."

Kirkpatrick frowned at him. A knock at the door jerked Wentworth's head that way. He was impatient, but summoned the person to enter. Jenkyns bowed himself in with a portable phone in his hands.

"Call for the Commissioner, sir," he said apologetically.

Kirkpatrick took the instrument with a swift, irritated gesture, spoke his name into the transmitter. Then abruptly irritation fled from his face and his eyes gleamed like agate. "I'll be right up," he promised.

He handed the phone to Jenkyns and turned his brilliant blue eyes on Wentworth.

"Another crucifixion," he snapped, "and that's not the worst of it!"

Wentworth jerked to his feet, lips tight with horror. Had they found Caroline Davis, and murdered her, or—

"A party of five people was on the sidewalk in front of the house when they ran out," Kirkpatrick said coldly, his voice utterly without expression. "The killers tossed a bomb among them. Four are dead. The fifth—the fifth lost both her legs."

A HOARSE curse rasped from Wentworth. These killers were utterly without mercy. Five people murdered simply because they stood on the sidewalk before a house! Murdered horribly—blown to bits! These murderers must be wiped out, quickly, before they drove the entire city mad with fear.

"Who was crucified?" he asked slowly and his lips were dry.

He had promised protection to Caroline Davis. If the killers had reached her before she could get clear of the building....

"A boy," Kirkpatrick said heavily. "A boy who sold papers and slept in one of the halls. No one knows his name except that he was called Micky, and... Damn those rats!" His anger blazed forth. "They take a kid like that who never harmed a soul in his life and kill him with horrible torture. And why? Why?"

Kirkpatrick choked off his rage, forced himself to calmness with tense lips and narrowed eyes.

"There are witnesses," he said slowly. Wentworth's eyes burned into the Police Commissioner's. "What do they say?"

Kirkpatrick shook his head heavily. "It sounds... Well, three women and a man who were looking out of a window across the street say that a hunchbacked man in a black cloak threw the bomb. He laughed and laughed as the car drove away, the same crazy laughing that was heard at the other crucifixions."

Wentworth cried, "What!" He was hoarse. He half-feared to hear what would come next. Had the gangsters dared to....

"Dick," Kirkpatrick swallowed noisily, shook his head again. "Dick, they say that the hunchbacked man was—the Spider!"

CHAPTER 3
THE KILLERS AGAIN

THOUGH HE was burning with eagerness to renew the battle with the ruthless murder gang, Wentworth declined Kirkpatrick's invitation to join the investigation of the crimes. He was fairly trembling with anger. Not content with their two thwarted attempts to kill the Spider, the Murder Master had loosed another and indirect attack upon him. He would hang his fearful crimes upon Wentworth!

Wentworth forced himself to calmness. He had fought before against gangsters who sought to blame the Spider for their infamy, but never had he battled men who struck so swiftly and with such precision. He jerked his head sharply. He must not let anger work on him like *this*. He must lay his plans and strike back, strike terribly. He strode to a phone, dialed the number of Nita van Sloan, the one woman in the world who knew of his high pledge of service, who knew that Richard Wentworth was the Spider!

He was frowning as he listened to the mechanical clicks and buzzes of the instrument. Nita often assisted him in his work, but there would be no joy in her heart at word of this latest battle. Wentworth had only recently regained his full strength after being shot down in another fight with the underworld. During his convalescence, Nita and he had been much together, stealing a few moments of happiness from the years of struggle and death which lay behind and ahead of him. And now, all this too brief felicity would end—because of a new duel with murder and crime with a criminal beside whom, all others seemed mild and weak.

The operations of this Master Brain had almost overwhelmed him, had almost eliminated the Spider from the battle. It was such things as this which kept Wentworth and Nita from consummating their great love in marriage. Wentworth would not take a wife and bring into the world children upon whose innocent heads might fall the disgrace of the Spider's downfall.

Yet, despite his great service to humanity, his downfall could bring only disgrace. The law could not consider the motives of his many executions of justice. Though his kills benefited mankind, to the law they were, and must always remain, simply murder. Furthermore, Wentworth had no illusions as to his own super-abilities. He knew that he was strong and quick; that his brain was nearly always equal to the demands he placed upon it. But some day, the Spider would falter—as he so nearly had fallen this night. Some day his enemies or the police would trap the Spider, and on that day he wanted no one save himself to suffer.

No, he could never marry Nita. He had fought violently against love of her, but the emotion had been greater than their combined strength. So they had bowed to the inevitable, snatching what moments of happiness might be theirs; working together when the needs of humanity called the Spider forth once more to battle for its rights.

Wentworth smiled as he heard the blurred sleepiness of Nita's voice. She was instantly awake when she knew who had called.

"What is it, Dick?" she asked quickly, and much as she strove to keep her fears and apprehensions from him, he detected her alarm.

"You know the case I was working on," he said simply. "It has developed unexpected angles. They have tried tonight twice within an hour to kill me." He broke off to laugh. "Well, those who tried it won't again, my sweet. I want you to go to the Martha Washington Hotel first thing in the morning, find Frances Richards there and stay with her. She is really Caroline Davis and I think she may prove valuable. Tell her that you received a mysterious summons from the Spider, that you admire the man—if I'm not asking you to perjure yourself, dearest?"

WENTWORTH LAUGHED again, picturing Nita's lovely face with its eyes of velvety blue, the sleep-fluffed bronze of her chestnut curls. She was telling him in emphatic tones that he was impossible, that he was a supreme egotist, but yes, maybe she did *admire* him a little....

His laughter died when she asked what he intended to do.

"I'm getting out of this apartment for one thing," he said briefly. "They've found me and I don't intend to have my movements hampered by surveillance. I'll keep in touch."

He hung up slowly, touched a bell at his side and old Jenkyns bowed from the doorway, his eyes worried. "Ram Singh and Jackson?" Wentworth queried.

Jenkyns shook his white head. "They have not yet returned, sir."

"The devil!" Wentworth bounded to his feet. A full hour had passed since he had reached the apartment, since the killers had penetrated the guard of his faithful servants and attacked him. Their failure to return could mean only that they had run afoul of the same net that had nearly snared him. Truly, the Murder Master was thorough.

Even as he thought these things, Wentworth was striding across the room. A tap at his holsters had assured him his guns were in place. He shrugged into a top-coat, raced from the building. He had to walk down two floors and take the public elevator because his own was not yet repaired.

He spent a frantic hour in search, finally tried the Morgue and the hospitals. It was in the latter that he located his two faithful men, both being treated for the injuries they suffered when an automobile had slammed at full speed into theirs as they were following Wentworth home. Ram Singh was still unconscious, but Jackson had regained his senses, asked pardon for their inefficiency with pale, scarcely moving lips.

Wentworth jerked his hand impatiently. "You did your best, Jackson," he said. "You always do. There is no question of pardon. Do you know who rammed you? Did you get any chance to see their faces?"

Jackson nodded weakly. "I wasn't knocked out until after the crash," he said. "I staggered out and two men came at me with blackjacks. I tore off a guy's pocket…" He reached fumblingly toward his pillow.

Wentworth groped beneath it, drew out a patch-pocket of brown tweed and a folded scrap of paper. He scanned the fragment eagerly. It read:

Guard Columbus until 2 a.m. At 3 a.m. cover Robert Kenton.

Wentworth started at that name. Kenton was one of the richest of the city's younger capitalists, a power in the nation's financial councils. Did the machinations of this Master Killer touch him, too? He glanced at his watch. Two forty-five already.

"You did well, Jackson," he commended the sick man. "I'm leaving instructions for your care. You'll be out in a few days,

39

CAROLINE DAVIS

SIDNEY CARTWRIGHT

JACK HAYES

HARRY BOISE

PHINEAS
MERRIWELL

EMILE
BOWFEE

they say. Ram Singh isn't badly hurt either. I'm leaving my apartment. Look for orders from Jenkyns."

He stalked hurriedly from the hospital, drove northward along Fifth Avenue toward the expensive apartment that Robert Kenton maintained for his town-house opposite Central Park. His mind was racing with the implications of what he had learned. The slip of paper was obviously the instructions of a gangster leader to his subordinate, and proved the masterly organization of the killers.

It was obvious that they had a system of guards for each hideout and job. The men who had wrecked Ram Singh's car had been on the watch at the Columbus stronghold. Probably, though, they had not been the same that had attempted to bomb him in his home. Such organization would call for a bomb squad and a flanking convoy to take out opposition.

Wentworth smiled grimly. He had met ruthless and thorough enemies before, but never such as *this*. Some fearsome plan must be under way since they dared thus to carry the battle to the Spider. Some plan—but what? What was behind these fearful crimes—these wholesale killings? Was there any connection between the crucifixion murders and this reference to Robert Kenton in a note snatched from a killer's clothing?

KIRKPATRICK'S INFORMATION about the building plans had hinted at a possible motive for the crucifixions on the site of the skyscraper. But, as the Commissioner said, business men did not usually resort to murder, however near they might come to the limits of the law. He broke into his own thoughts to scan the shadows of the side streets past which his powerful Hispano-Suiza purred. He was only two blocks from Robert Kenton's apartment now. The young financier occupied the top three floors of that sleek white building that reared itself just ahead. There were lights on a terrace on the east side.

Wentworth whirled into an entrance of the park, sought out one of the secluded parking places that open darkly off the drives and halted his car there. He went to work then, resuming the Spider disguise. The master of these Torture Killers should learn to dread his cloaked, hunch-backed figure, Wentworth swore to himself with thinning lips. Whatever the killers' business tonight could be, it would be the Spider in recognizable garb who interfered—if he were not already too late.

Silent as the fall of darkness, he stole across the grassy stretch, which, spotted with shrubbery and low trees, separated him from Fifth Avenue. He saw no shadow which might be a man on watch, detected no cruising or parked cars. Was it possible that he was too late? From three o'clock on, the note had said, the guards were to patrol. It was now but a quarter past three… Wentworth crossed the street quickly, a hunched queer figure in draped black, and stole into the main entrance. A *chasseur* sat with nodding head upon a marble bench. His faint snoring was not interrupted by the Spider's silent passage into Kenton's private elevator.

The cage moved upward soundlessly. The foyer of the capital-ist's apartment, opening directly from the elevator, was carpeted in luxurious silken rugs. Bowls of drooping vines reflected yellow light against the ceiling, shed soft illumination. Wentworth stood unmoving, his keen eyes flicking over the expensive over-furnishing of the lounge. Three doors opened from it, and all were closed. He found a moment later that all were locked also, but that presented no serious barrier to the Spider.

He selected the midmost door and a small steel probe with a right-angle bend at its tip slid from the ever-ready tool kit strapped compactly beneath his arm. Within moments, the lock clicked dully and he manipulated the knob with slender sensitive fingers that were carefully gloved to prevent leaving prints.

The door moved soundlessly. No disturbing noise came from within. Yet Wentworth hesitated. Everything had been too easy. It was not like the Master of the Torture Killers to make things so easy for an enemy—unless he wanted him to enter. There was that doorway which had dropped a steel portcullis and turned a hallway into a murder trap. A quick glance behind him revealed nothing suspicious. The elevator still showed a gleam of orange light behind its wood-paneled doorway. The other two doors that opened into the foyer were blank. Wentworth jerked his head, half angrily. This Master Killer was testing his nerves with constant, unrelenting, hidden attacks.

He shoved the door inward softly, slid in and eased it shut again, peering about quickly. A great room with bare gleaming floors gave upon the east terrace; Wentworth had seen the lights from the street. The room curved around to the left. He glided forward, peered up its length—then bounded forward with a cry he could scarcely suppress.

Against a high fireplace a white inert form dangled. A head of soft blonde hair sagged forward and the golden tresses spilled across straining shoulders. The arms were stretched upward at an angle; the fingers were clenched and a tracery of black blood made them horrible. Before the hearth, a great winged chair was drawn by girdled ropes, but Wentworth paid that no heed as he sprang to the side of the tortured girl. Two things thudded home into his brain like bullet shocks. The girl, stripped naked and crucified, nailed by the palms of her hands to the heavy wooden mantel, was dead! She had the seal of the Spider on her forehead!

A FURY of anger made Wentworth's body rigid. He cursed raspingly, whirled toward the chair looped with rope. There was a man there, naked to the waist. His torso had been slashed in a criss-cross pattern of torture. Great burned splotches were traced among them. And he, too, was dead, with the seal of the Spider imprinted upon his forehead!

Wentworth saw the whole fearful story as if he had been a witness to it. The man—it was Robert Kenton, youngest giant of Wall Street—had been tortured for some information which he would not yield. Finally, the killers had hit upon the fiendish plan of torturing Kenton's daughter before his eyes. She probably had come in late from some entertainment—the shreds of her evening dress lay upon the floor. It was likely they had obtained their information then, and out of sheer mad torture-lust, had killed the girl and her father.

Wentworth was trembling with the rage that burned within him. A sick horror gnawed at his brain. This lovely girl with her strained, virginal breasts had suffered horribly before she had died. It was written large upon her face. The nails had torn her palms before a knife had let out her life. What, in God's name, was behind these fiendish murders? Who was the Master Killer who—The door slammed inward against the wall with a crash like thunder.

Wentworth spun, his hand raking for his gun, then flung himself face downward as he saw that the men who were piling through the doorway wore the blue uniform of New York's police. Against such as these, the Spider's guns were mute.

"It's the Spider!" a cop shouted hoarsely. "Kill the murdering skunk!"

Guns belched deadly lead, but Wentworth was crouched behind the chair that held the body of Robert Kenton. Not only were these two persons, terribly dead, branded with his seal, but the Spider himself was caught on the scene of the crime. The fact that this man and girl had been dead for hours would not save him. Hours dead! Then....

Wentworth's lips snarled back from his teeth.

He saw now the truth of that note that Jackson had "snatched" from the killer. It had been planted in that loyal man's hand on the chance that the Spider would escape the bomber. During the battle in the Columbus Avenue stronghold, the Master Killer had had time to estimate possibilities, had been able to plan this trap to snare him should all others fail.

A bullet scraped past the arm of the chair and its hot breath fanned Wentworth's cheek. He crouched lower. The police were spreading out to take him on the flanks. He could not fire back, yet he must escape. He alone even suspected the existence of the Murder Master. If he did not break from this trap to thwart the man, heaven only knew what atrocities he might contrive.

He must escape, but how? A bullet bored through the chair arm, plucked at his hat brim from the left. The police had almost completed their encircling movement. Within seconds, their lead would find the Spider....

WENTWORTH WRENCHED his head about to seek a way out. The great fireplace yawned behind him with Kenton's daughter dangling white and stark across it. To the right, ten feet distant, was a door that gave on the terrace. If only he could reach that—

A bullet hissed past, struck the girl's leg. The body swayed, did a gruesome, stiff-jointed dance. Wentworth opened his mouth and screamed, screamed like a woman in pain, then his voice dropped to a faint whisper.

"Don't," he pleaded in a girl's light tones. "In God's name…" He was not ten feet from that body that had swayed to the thudding weight of a bullet. The accents were those of a woman weak with agony.

His scream spread cursing consternation among the police. Their guns were instantly silent.

"She's still alive!" a man said violently. "In God's name, stop that shooting!"

"Yes, she's still alive," Wentworth cried out sharply. "Those nail-holes in her hands won't kill her for a long time—unless you keep me penned up here and let her die!"

"You murdering devil!" The unseen officer's voice was hoarse with rage.

"I didn't nail her up there," Wentworth declared forcefully. "I was about to take her down when you blundering fools crashed

47

in. You're going to cause her death if you don't get out. I won't surrender, so I hope you won't be stubborn—for Miss Kenton's sake."

Bleak silence fell when he ceased speaking. After a moment, Wentworth could hear the men whispering together, but their voices were too excited for him to make out words.

"This is the work of the torture killers," Wentworth said again. "They're trying to blame me for it; you're helping by sticking around. Get outside the room and close the door and I'll take the girl down. Otherwise—"

He broke off, and once more moaned like a woman in pain. "Please," he gasped faintly. "Oh, please...."

"We're going out," snarled the unseen man's voice, "but you needn't think we believe your lies, or that we'll let you get away. We...."

"Hurry!" Wentworth snapped, "or the girl will die."

Heavy feet trod to the door. Wentworth waited until he heard the portal shut, then he shot out the lights with his air-pistol. He heard a startled gasp of breath and smiled grimly. He had expected the police would leave a man to pick him off, but the dark would make his task difficult. Without an instant's delay, he dashed to the terrace door. He whirled around the jamb, gripped with clinging fingers as he hurled past. Inside the room a gun crashed out.

The lead splintered the casing around which he swung, whined harmlessly off into the night. For the moment Wentworth was safe. But already the hall door had crashed open. Police would stream out into the darkened terrace....

Wentworth found a casement open and dived through it, back into the house. Somewhere in the apartment would be servants' quarters. If he could only find them before police reached the spot, there still was a chance of escape. He padded silently along a dimly lighted hall, peering into rooms. Finally he found the servants' quarters and here, too, was death. A man lay crumpled upon the floor, the back of his head crushed in. A servant-girl had been strangled, a Chinese cook was almost beheaded. God, was there no end to the fiendishness of these killers! A sick rage writhed in his breast, but Wentworth could not delay even to sorrow for these dead innocents.

THE DEAD man wore only trousers and shirt, house-slippers on his feet. Wentworth dragged him into a closet, stuffed the make-up of the Spider upon a shelf. It would not condemn him, a simple servant.

Deliberately then, Wentworth stripped to shirt and trousers smeared his forehead with blood from the unconscious servant's wounds. He whirled, staggered out into the hallway.

"Police!" he cried Hoarsely. "Police! Burglar! Mr. Kenton! Burglars!"

A policeman slammed out into the hall with a leveled revolver. Wentworth stumbled toward him with joyful cries. "Officer! Officer!" he gasped. "Burglars!"

The man shoved a broad hand against Wentworth's chest. "Slow up," he growled. "Who the hell are you?"

"The butler, sir," Wentworth gasped. "Mr. Kenton's butler. Some men broke into my room, hit me over the head, and…."

The cop barked. "Come in here."

He paced back down the hall toward the main entrance to the apartment/ "Sweeney!" he yelled "Oh, Sweeney, look what I got!"

As they reached the main entrance, Wentworth swung his right fist, starting it low at his side. It cracked behind the policeman's ear and he went down hard. Sweeney hadn't answered the man's cry. Probably Sweeney was one of the group hunting the Spider. Wentworth stripped off the policeman's overcoat hastily. He slapped the visored cap on his own head, ran to the exit while he shrugged into the overcoat. He fastened the last button, and the officer's service revolver in his hand, slammed out into the hall.

"Quick," he shouted to the two officers on guard. "Sweeney wants help. I'm going for bombs."

He sprang to the elevator and the men charged into the apartment. There was a policeman on guard in the lower hall, but Wentworth stalked past him with only a gesture of greeting and faded a few moments later into the shadows of the street. He tossed the policeman's coat and cap into an alley and circled to where he had left his car in Central Park.

It was broad daylight when he registered at a hotel and sent for the morning papers. They had nothing about the Robert Kenton case—it had broken too late—but it still brought him news of the Torture Killers. Police, hot on the trail of the crucifixion of a boy in the block of buildings where a skyscraper was to rise, had gone back over the list of witnesses in the former crimes. In each case there had been at least one man or woman who would swear the Spider had committed the murders. They had been afraid to talk before, they said, but police were protecting them now. Their names were kept secret. Wentworth smiled grimly as he read this news. If he needed further proof of the might of the Master Criminal he battled, this supplied it.

As never before, the police would howl on the trail of the Spider. His enemies hoped to hamper him so that he would be helpless to battle them. There was superb planning in every phase of this Murder Master's activities. The attacks upon the Spider had been executed with perfect precision. Here was a man who planned ahead, even as Wentworth himself did—who weighed all contingencies and prepared in advance to turn them to his own advantage.

But Wentworth's eternal vigilance had saved him. He had escaped all the traps, and now he must prepare his own counter-attack. His lips thinned bitterly. Heaven help him if he miscalculated by so much as an atom's width. If he did, this Murder Master would smash him. If only, he could find the purpose of these killers, it would help. However much the murder of Robert Kenton obscured the original clue, he must follow down the first three crucifixion murders which had brought him into the case. **BUT WAIT,** didn't he, Wentworth, know a motive for the murder of Kenton and his daughter and the needless slaughter of the servants? He recalled that there had been a fight among three groups to control Atlas Mutual, one of the nation's richest companies, a fight that even yet was undecided. And Kenton was an Atlas vice-president and a big stock holder. Wentworth started to his feet, smacked a clenched fist into a palm.

Was it possible? Good Lord, it must be! Those first murders might have been actuated by a desire to buy land cheaply for a huge corporation. This murder of Kenton must have been to obtain information that would help in the battle for control of Atlas. Then it meant that the Murder Master was working through crime and the underworld to dominate in commerce!

In a flash, Wentworth saw the potentialities of such a conspiracy. An unscrupulous man who did not fear to murder to achieve his ends could readily wipe out all opposition in business and make himself a virtual czar of industry. He could set up monopolies, hi-jack the control of companies, bankrupt enemies. He could set fire to wealthy buildings insured by a rival firm and rain claims upon it. Human lives meant nothing to him. Human fortunes even less. He....

Wentworth rolled the newspapers into a club and flung it across the room. He strode from the hotel, sought a telephone through which he could not be traced and called Nita at the Martha Washington Hotel. He must see Caroline Davis and question her at length. It was possible she might recall something that would give him a clue to the murderers who had seized upon her as prey. He must not lose a minute in his attack on the Murder Master, for there was no way of telling where the blow would fall next.

When Wentworth said: "Hello, darling," Nita gasped.

"Oh, Dick!" she cried, then hushed her words, whispering so that Wentworth, crowding the receiver against his ear, could barely hear. "Stanley Kirkpatrick called me an hour ago and I've been trying everywhere since then to reach you. The police say the Spider killed Robert Kenton."

"I know," Wentworth interrupted. "It was a trick...."

"But, Dick," Nita broke in. "That isn't all. Witnesses identified the Spider as…" Her voice faded, a faint sob came over the wire.

"As whom?" Wentworth snapped.

"They swore, Dick, that they recognized the Spider and that—that *you are the Spider!*"

CHAPTER 4
INTO THE TRAP!

WENTWORTH CURSED once savagely, deep in his throat. For a full minute he was silent, then he requested details. Nita gave them in a rush. Three persons had seen him entering the apartment building where Robert Kenton lived, the story ran. One of them had seen him disguising himself as the Spider—had identified him positively.

It was obvious that this was another of the attacks upon Wentworth by the Murder Master. The enemy was merciless and cunning in his work. He would give the Spider no rest, no opportunity to strike back. Even when he was hidden from them, the assaults continued.

"What, precisely, did Kirkpatrick say?" Wentworth asked slowly.

"He said," Nita quoted, "tell Dick that when I find him I shall arrest him myself. The evidence is overwhelming."

Wentworth nodded slowly once. Kirkpatrick had risked his job to send him that warning. Yet it was clear to Wentworth the Commissioner suspected trickery in the evidence, for he would have cut off his hand rather than fail in any jot of his duty. Then the evidence must be such that he was being forced to act, though convinced of its falsity. And he knew the importance of the Spider remaining at liberty when such crimes were occurring.

Wentworth nodded again at the thought. That was the solution, he knew. But Kirkpatrick's conviction that the evidence was false would not help him. The Commissioner would be forced to act—if he found him.

He had wanted to make sure that he would not find Wentworth.

"Have you learned anything more important?"

Wentworth asked calmly, fighting agitation from his voice.

"I don't think so," Nita said. "I think that if I can help you, I know a safe place to put Caroline Davis. Then I could come to you and—"

Wentworth frowned. "I'm afraid, Nita," he said over the phone, "there's nothing you could do right now better than watch over her. And keep in touch with Kirk."

"But Caroline is secretly engaged to Phineas Merriwell's adopted son. You know the man I mean, Phineas Merriwell, the millionaire? She would be safe at his home," Nita was pleading.

Wentworth knew Merriwell, but he wanted to keep Nita out of this battle as much as possible. Already the enemy had stripped him of Ram Singh and Jackson. Nita might very well be next.

"I'll think it over," he agreed finally. "But meantime, keep in touch with things. I'll call you back soon." He hooked the receiver back in its cradle.

From the drug store phone-booth, Wentworth turned to a restaurant, entered the men's room. There, with nimble hands, he went to work on his face. His cheek bones broadened so that his still-swollen eyes became less conspicuous. His hair was crisp and black, parted precisely on the left. He raked it into a ruff which a swift, swabbing of soap made stiff. And when he walked from the rest room, he moved with a shuffling swagger that took the arrogant self-reliance from his poise. During the next half-hour, he reinforced his disguise by purchases at clothing stores, replacing his brown fedora with a gray cap, his natty tailored clothing with loud ready-mades.

WENTWORTH CONTRIVED a very careful disguise, for he intended going to Police headquarters when it was complete. The plot to frame him was a much more direct lead to the Torture Killers than he might get by questioning Caroline Davis. If he could identify the witnesses against himself, who had sworn they saw him enter the apartment building without a disguise; if he could force those witnesses to reveal the person who had bought their testimony, he might reach the Murder Master.

But first, there was another clue he wanted to trace briefly: the clue of the corporation which was purchasing buildings to raze for a skyscraper site, the corporation which stood to profit by the crucifixion killings.

From newspaper clippings, he gleaned information that one Sidney Cartwright, lawyer, was representative for the corporation that planned the skyscraper. Wentworth frowned over that information. He knew the attorney slightly, knew his reputation thoroughly. He was a corporation counsel of excellent repute; apparently possessed of considerable private means.

Cartwright spent a great deal more time at the estates of the wealthy, at various exclusive beach clubs than he did at his office. Wentworth often had seen his curly blond hair, his lean browned body—Cartwright would never, regardless of fashion, have worn anything but trunks upon a beach. His chest and back were superbly muscled—as the lawyer sprawled on the sands or, cleaving the air in a clean dive, streaked through the waters with perfect stroke and rhythm. The man was well liked in feminine circles where his shrewd face with its high sweep of sun-tanned forehead was frequently seen.

Wentworth shrugged. The man did not seem a likely suspect, but the trail pointed that way. Before this he had found criminals in unlikely places. Perhaps he might obtain a clue from one of Cartwright's clients.

Wentworth looked up from his clippings and was aware that his eyes were smarting. He rubbed them absently, glanced in a pocket mirror as he crossed to the phone, then stopped and inspected his face closely. The swelling certainly had not diminished. If anything, it had increased. He frowned and went to the phone. That tear-gas must certainly have been powerful stuff. Ordinarily, its effect would have faded long ago. His call went through, and Eddie Blanton of the *Press* answered.

"What's the lowdown on Sidney Cartwright?"

Wentworth asked. "He's got a deal on he wants me to tie up with."

The newspaper man dragged out a "We-e-ll, it's a little hard to say. Cartwright represents the boss sometimes."

"Bowfee?" Wentworth asked.

His friend gave assent. Emile Bowfee was the publisher of the *Press,* together with many other newspapers strung from coast to coast. He had roared his deep-chested way to millions through the columns of his papers as a crusader against injustice and crime. Bowfee had been the first editor to prohibit the over-display of crime news on the from page; he had issued a flat edict against the heroizing of gangsters.

"They're rats, everyone of them," Bowfee had declared. "When you play them up or talk about a man preserving the underworld code of silence, you're just breeding potential criminals in the children of today."

WENTWORTH'S FROWN increased. Nothing that he had learned supported his theories about Cartwright, but he was still positive there must be a connection between the purchase of a building site and the crucifix murders. He determined to investigate the lawyer further, but meantime he would see Kirkpatrick. Wentworth took a Broadway street car southward and, an hour after he had received the warning call from Nita, he shambled with slight, rolling swagger up the broad steps of Police Headquarters. He took off his gray cap as he sidled into the presence of the desk sergeant. He ducked his head and looked up deferentially under his brows.

"What d'ya want?" the sergeant snapped at him. "I seen something," Wentworth said awkwardly.

"I seen something I think you ought to know, Captain."

The sergeant peered at him suspiciously.

Wentworth's dress and manner was that which would always win glances from the police. He looked like a professional "hard guy."

"What did you see?" the sergeant demanded. Wentworth dragged a newspaper from his pocket and pointed to the headlines about Kenton, tapped a picture of the murdered financier with a grimy forefinger.

"I know where that guy lives," Wentworth said, "and last night I saw a hunchback guy in a black cape go into his house, and...."

The sergeant spun from his chair at the desk, stalked around to Wentworth's side. He caught him by the arm with powerful fingers as if afraid he would run away.

"Hi, Bill!" he yelled, "go up and tell the Commissioner I got another witness fer him!"

Wentworth was ushered with precipitate haste into the presence of Stanley Kirkpatrick. He stood awkwardly, both hands running about the edge of the cap. He stared at the floor, met Kirkpatrick's eyes only in little frightened glances, when he jerked his gaze from its wanderings about the room. Kirkpatrick's face was set, his mouth a thin line beneath the waxed points of his mustache. His eyes were bitter.

"You may go, Flannahan," he told the sergeant and not another word did he utter until the door was closed behind the officer. Even then he only stared fixedly at Wentworth. Kirkpatrick had both elbows on his desk and he tapped his right fist against his left palm again and again.

"What's your story?" he asked sharply.

"Jeez, boss," Wentworth whined. "I don't want no trouble. I just seen this story in the paper and I knowed what I seen. So I comes in like a good citizen to tell what I knows."

"What's your story?" Kirkpatrick repeated coldly. Wentworth pulled his eyes from a far corner of the room and let them flick across Kirkpatrick's strong demanding face. Never had he seen the Commissioner so grim. He opened his mouth to speak, then hesitated as the door behind him opened quietly.

"I've requested you to notify me when you have more witnesses on the Kenton case," spoke a voice which Wentworth recognized—the edged, threatening voice of Howard Boise, the District Attorney's assistant.

Kirkpatrick snapped to his feet. "Get *this,* Boise," he said, biting out each word as if from metal. "I'm still running this department and I do as I see fit. Now keep your mouth shut, or get out of here."

WENTWORTH TWISTED about to stare at the pale, sharp face of the attorney. He allowed his mouth to hang open as if he could not conceive of any man defying the Police Commissioner. He turned back to Kirkpatrick, then rolled his shoulders back.

"Say the word, chief," he husked, "and I'll bounce him outa here fer youse."

Kirkpatrick stared at Wentworth, and his grim lips twitched at the corners. For once Wentworth's eyes did not dance about the room, and he saw in that instant that the Commissioner

He fanned three more bullets in among the
chemical bottles—then ducked from sight.

had recognized him. Hell, that was bad! Suppose Kirkpatrick considered it his duty to arrest....

"That will be quite unnecessary, my man," Kirkpatrick said. "Just go ahead with the story you were telling me when this gentleman—interrupted."

Wentworth stared at Kirkpatrick a moment longer, then stepped back and began to roll his cap again. He eased out a deep breath. Kirkpatrick intended to carry the show on. It was clear that Boise had some power, some authority that forced the Commissioner to permit such interference—either that, or Kirkpatrick had hidden reasons for leading Boise on.

"Geez," said Wentworth. "I don't wanna cause no trouble, but I seen this piece in the paper…" He told once more the story that he had given the desk sergeant.

"Could you identify the hunch-backed man?" Kirkpatrick asked.

"Well, now, I'll tell youse," said Wentworth wagging his head. "I don't like to say a thing I ain't sure about. But this guy looked exactly like the newspapers say this here Spider looks."

Kirkpatrick was seated again, once more tapping his fist against his palm. Boise had paced across the room and his expressionless, long-jawed face was turned alertly toward Wentworth.

"You see, Commissioner," Boise said sharply. "There is no doubt about it any longer. When man after man comes into the office and tells you it was this Spider!"

"That's just what I don't like about it," Kirkpatrick objected. "There's too much volunteer information. Man, don't forget that the Spider is a terror! There isn't one man in a hundred who would testify against him, ordinarily, yet we here have four volunteers who identify him out of hand."

Wentworth listened to Kirkpatrick's harangue, realized anew what intelligence and swift cleverness were combined in this Commissioner of Police who was his friend. Kirkpatrick already had perceived the reason for his visit, and while apparently arguing with Boise, was giving him the information he had come to obtain. He was explaining just now why he had phoned the alarm to Nita.

"These people saw what they say they did," Boise snapped. "You can't challenge the word of that old woman and man; you can't doubt Sidney Cartwright."

Wentworth barely suppressed the start that jerked at his muscles at mention of the lawyer's name. So Cartwright was one of the witnesses against him! No wonder the commissioner had doubted the authenticity of the information, especially since it had been Kirkpatrick himself who had broached the purchases of land by Cartwright as a possible hidden motive for the crucifixion murders!

"How Cartwright could swear not only that this man was the Spider, but also that he was Richard Wentworth, I cannot understand," Kirkpatrick said argumentatively. "The police know definitely that this hunch-backed figure is a disguise that the Spider assumes only on occasions when he wishes to be recognized. I cannot see how Cartwright could penetrate that disguise. Furthermore, I don't believe that if the Spider staged a double murder, he would do it in a disguise that everyone would recognize on sight."

WENTWORTH ONLY half-heard Kirkpatrick's explanation, a summary of additional reasons for doubting the information he had received. That was what the Commissioner was giving him. But he was doing more than that. He was proving that Sidney Cartwright was one of the Torture Killers, probably the head of that fearful band. The trail Wentworth had followed and the clue of the accusations against him both pointed to the same trail—and that trail led directly to the door of Sidney Cartwright!

He had all the information he wanted now. It only remained for him to get clear of headquarters and attack. The escape might be difficult, as matters lay now. The assistant District Attorney probably would insist that he be held on high bail as a material witness. Wentworth had not calculated on Boise's presence. He edged toward the door while Boise argued with Kirkpatrick and got his hand on the knob....

The door slammed inward with a speed that whirled Wentworth aside. True to his disguise, he danced on his toes like a stumbling prize-fighter, his fists half-rising in self defense, then he dropped his hands and let his mouth sag open. The man who stood in the doorway was tall and broad with smooth black hair. His hooked nose was thinned dangerously and his small black eyes snapped. For a minute he stood there, then he stalked into the room with bouncing small strides: the mayor of New York!

Boise whirled and a dry, brittle smile crossed his lips. Kirkpatrick got slowly to his feet, frowning. Wentworth's thoughts were whirling. Why did the mayor of New York come to Kirkpatrick's office? He knew the mayor hated Kirkpatrick, had retained him only because of Kirkpatrick's immense efficiency and popularity. He detected a fierce gloating on the mayor's face as he pounded up to the desk, leaned over it and slapped a palm hard upon its surface.

"Mr. Kirkpatrick," the mayor bit out. "You are suspended from office pending trial on charges that you have violated your oath of office. You may *also* find yourself charged with being accessory to the murder of Robert Kenton!"

Kirkpatrick stiffened angrily. His face was a mirror of contempt for the politician who had won office as the city's mayor.

"You will explain those remarks," he said stiffly, "or I'll...."

"I'll explain, them," the mayor howled. "I'll explain, them, all right. You sent word to Wentworth; that he was wanted for murder. And now Wentworth has disappeared!"

He slammed his fist on the desk. "I've got you where I want you now, Kirkpatrick. You've overplayed your hand. You telephoned a warning to Wentworth. That makes you accessory to murder for helping him escape!"

The Mayor spun toward Boise, who had a thin, cruel grin on his sharp, white face.

"Boise, you will act as Police Commissioner until after the trial. After that, I think I can promise you the job permanently!"

CHAPTER 5
THE SPIDER GOES CALLING

INTENT ON escape, Wentworth was already sliding toward the door when the mayor's voice rang out triumphantly. It stopped him dead in his tracks, torn by indecision. It was imperative that he flee from police headquarters and this interruption offered him a perfect opportunity—yet Kirkpatrick was in this jam solely because he had attempted to help his friend. A word from Wentworth would clear Kirkpatrick and imprison him.

Wentworth's hands clenched at his sides, his jaw set. He cast a glance toward the outer office. It was empty. There was no obstacle to his get-away. Still he hesitated. Should he reveal his own identity, say that Kirkpatrick's message had been only to advise him to surrender, say that he had come in disguise because he wished to surrender directly to the Commissioner? That would confound the Mayor's charges utterly.

On the other hand, if Wentworth surrendered, it would leave only the police to combat the gigantic commercial conspiracy which threatened the lives and fortunes of thousands of people. He would save Kirkpatrick, but the city would be at the mercy of the Torture Killers. The Spider's lips twisted sardonically. As always, his duty to humanity ran counter to the dictates of his heart. There could be but one decision. He must escape and hope to help Kirkpatrick later.

Wentworth moved again toward the doorway, yet hesitated, to listen a moment longer to the Mayor's gloating over Kirkpatrick. The Commissioner's face was set and angry.

"Who accuses me?" he demanded, and his voice was brittle.

The Mayor's full-lipped mouth smiled happily.

"Some one neither you nor anyone else can impeach," he said jubilantly. "A man of the highest integrity."

"Who accuses me?" Kirkpatrick demanded again.

"Sidney Cartwright!" The Mayor flung the name like a challenge.

Wentworth heard it with a start. One more count against

Cartwright—against the man behind the skyscraper corporation, and apparently, the Torture Murders. Cartwright feared the Police Commissioner might balk his schemes, had deliberately plotted his removal. There could be no doubt of it.

A thin smile disturbed Wentworth's mouth. It was time that the Spider paid a call on Cartwright. Without waiting for more words, Wentworth slipped from the office and walked quietly out of the building. He had made his choice. With such positive proof against Cartwright, he could no longer even consider sacrificing himself to help Kirkpatrick.

Wentworth shambled from the police station and found his way to a telephone from which he called Nita van Sloan again. "I'll need Ram Singh and Jackson tonight," he told her. "Kirk is in a tough spot, and…."

He broke off as Nita's coldly level voice interrupted. There was suppressed fury in her swift words. "The police have taken Ram Singh and Jackson," she said. "And they've gone after Jenkyns, too. All three are accused of withholding valuable information about you from the police."

"But they can't do that!" Wentworth cried. "That's not legal!"

Nita's short laugh was as cynical and hard as the Spider's could ever be.

"Boise arranged that," she said. "He put them under oath before a Grand Jury and held them for contempt when they refused to talk. They wouldn't plead that it might incriminate them because they didn't want to harm you by the implications of such a plea."

Rage flamed up within Wentworth, but his voice remained quiet.

"Thank you, Nita," he said. "If you get a chance to communicate with any of them, tell them to stick to that position. Get hold of my lawyer and get him to work releasing them. Keep Caroline Davis under cover. No, darling, you can help me most by carrying on just this way."

WENTWORTH PUSHED open the door of the booth, and two policemen stepped forward with leveled guns. A curse of amazement checked in his throat. He realized immediately what had happened. Nita's wires had been tapped and police had traced his call, raced here to arrest him.

"Hoist 'em, guy," snapped the nearest cop. "You're under arrest for...."

He shouted in fright then ducked back and squeezed the trigger of his revolver. Wentworth had gone into swift action. With a sideways leap, he had sprung clear of the muzzle of the gun. An out-thrown arm overturned a sales display of mineral oil. Quart bottles crashed noisily, smeared the floor with grease. The policeman's bullet pulverized a show case glass. Two clerks and several customers fled screaming to the street.

Wentworth's second leap flung him behind the prescription-counter and a second bullet smashed after him, spun a half dozen bottles from a shelf. A swift glance revealed that the trap door to the basement opened through the floor here. Wentworth groped for it with his left hand while he snaked out a gun from beneath his arm. He didn't shoot policemen, but a few well-directed bullets....

His first shot smashed an orange-drink container on the fountain and the sticky yellow liquid spewed. A second shot found a display of milk of magnesia. Then he had the trap door open. He fanned three more bullets in among the prescription chemical bottles, ducked into the basement and eased the trap door shut. It was the work of a moment to secure it, to dart across the cellar to a narrow window and muscle out into the open air.

Sirens were whining all about, but Wentworth was not spotted again as he shuffled along the street. He was frowning with thought. His first intention had been to race after Cartwright and force the man to talk. But if Cartwright were not the leader—and Wentworth suddenly doubted that the Master Killer would expose himself by accusing the Spider—then there was a further battle ahead. And Wentworth would need reinforcements. He could carry the physical warfare alone, but this commercial combine should be attacked also on the financial front. It would take a powerful and philanthropic man to risk his fortune in such a contest, and....

Abruptly he recalled Nita's report on Caroline Davis, that she was engaged to the adopted son of Phineas Merriwell, and Wentworth smiled. The man was fabulously wealthy. His name was behind many an anonymous million given to charity.

The aged millionaire was known to Wentworth both by name and reputation. Once he had seen the white-crowned old man being pushed along the street in his wheel chair by a Negro servant. It was Merriwell's habit to tour the slums and dole out pockets-full of bright new quarters. But he did not do it for publicity. He became infuriated if newspaper men approached.

Wentworth nodded. Phineas Merriwell was the man, and now was the time to enlist his work. Up to now, Wentworth's supposed connection with the Kenton murders had not been published. He could go in his own identity and seek to persuade Merriwell to help. He could tell him of the frame-up and use Caroline Davis as a basis of contact if he needed her. The decision made, Wentworth at once took a taxi for the Tarrytown home of the millionaire.

THROUGHOUT THE trip, Wentworth rode with eyes closed, behind smoked glasses. An eyewash had relieved them only temporarily. Merriwell had been adverse to the interview, but finally had assented. The butler reflected that attitude when he opened the door. He turned with a stiffly disapproving back and led Wentworth to a library where a great bay window showed the wide Hudson.

It was fifteen minutes before Phineas Merriwell entered, carried like a baby in the arms of a giant Negro. The servant's blankly black face seemed strange above the waved and plentiful white hair of the aged millionaire. Phineas Merriwell nodded cheerfully as he was gently deposited in his wheelchair before the window. The Negro stepped back and stood with folded arms. His eyes gazed straight ahead blankly.

Merriwell patted a blanket fussily about his knees, but his lips continued to smile, his pale-blue eyes were kindly behind the square-lensed glasses that gave his entire wrinkle-puckered face a strangely antique air. The millionaire could not be more than fifty-five, Wentworth knew, but he looked eighty save for the intense aliveness of his eyes.

"Now, Mr. Wentworth?" Merriwell began in a frail light voice. "You said that the welfare, perhaps the lives, of many people depended on your seeing me. I hope that you will be able to justify that claim. I dislike being imposed upon." He was suddenly fretful like a child. "My secretary is constantly allowing people to make silly claims upon my time."

"What I said was true," Wentworth said, studying the feeble old man. It was difficult to tell how to approach him. "I wonder if you read in the papers recently of some horrible murders in which persons were crucified?"

Merriwell's blue-veined hand toyed with a heavy gold watch-chain that looped across his vest.

"I suppose I did," he admitted, still fretfully. "I suppose so. But what possible connection...."

Wentworth drew a deep breath. The man's mind was keen enough he saw, despite the enfeeblement of his body. Rapidly, Wentworth explained the situation—how a frame-up had been directed at him for his efforts to frustrate the killers. He wound up by asking Merriwell to join forces with him against the criminals.

"I have nothing to do with business interests any more," Phineas Merriwell whined petulantly. "Even if I were willing to do anything like that, I'd have to consult my lawyer, Sidney Cartwright...."

Wentworth jerked to his feet with such a rush that Merriwell flung back in his chair and the Negro eyed him suspiciously.

"Good God!" Wentworth exclaimed, "Does Sidney Cartwright handle your business?"

Merriwell straightened slowly. "Yes, he does," he answered snappishly. "And I wish that the next time you decide to do something as suddenly as that, you'd let me know in advance. I'm not used...."

"Listen," Wentworth cut in. "Sidney Cartwright is the man I suspect of being tied up with this deal. He's handling the purchase of the building site where those murders were committed. He has accused me falsely, and... why, man, your money may be used to buy some of that land!"

"I don't think so," Merriwell fretted. "But I don't know. I'd have to consult my lawyer...."

"Do you mean," Wentworth asked, "that Sidney Cartwright holds your power of attorney? That he makes investments with your money without consulting you?" He was amazed and his surprise crept into his voice. Was it possible that a man of Merriwell's wealth and acumen would permit such a situation?

Merriwell jerked up his head. "What is that to you?" he demanded. "That is my private business. Cartwright is an honest man and a capable one. He takes better care of my money than I could."

WENTWORTH STARED through his smoked glasses at the old man. Merriwell was laying himself wide open to embezzlement and juggling of his funds. He might very well become subject to criminal prosecutions if Cartwright mishandled his funds in such a way as to involve him in the criminal activities of the Murder Master.

Wentworth heard the broad double doors open, jerked his head that way. A young man of twenty-four or five had entered, stood with his shoulders against the portal. Merriwell took no notice of him and Wentworth asked a sharp question.

"Tell me," he said, "How much loss have you suffered in real estate or stock deals recently?"

Merriwell stared at him with his intensely alive eyes, stared in surprise and interest. "How did you know?" he asked wonderingly. "I'm sure Cartwright wouldn't have talked about it to anyone, and...."

Wentworth was abruptly aware that the youth was striding toward them. "Oh, sir," he said, "can't you persuade father not to trust that man Cartwright any more? I am sure he's stealing his money and...."

"That will do, Arthur, that will do," Merriwell broke in. "I know you mean to help me, but you don't understand."

Wentworth looked from one to the other, the upstanding young man with his frank, open face, the petulant old millionaire. He knew who the youth was, of course. Merriwell had never married, but he had adopted six children of various ages, four girls and two boys. This was Arthur, the eldest, the one to whom Caroline Davis was engaged. His concerned affection was proof of his regard for old Phineas. It was useless, however, to ask Merriwell again for help. If he was guided solely by Cartwright, it would hinder more than help if he confided further in him.

Wentworth got abruptly to his feet. "Thank you, Mr. Merriwell," he said. "You have helped me more than you can know."

He was positive now that Cartwright was embezzling from this trustful old man. His guess on losses in dealings had been made in the dark, but it had revealed definitely, to his own way of thinking, that Cartwright was taking money and giving false explanations of what had happened to it. It put an entirely different aspect on the lawyer and lent credence to his beliefs. The youth's suspicions were an added confirmation.

He must find out where Cartwright was, and… "Please, Mr. Wentworth!" It was the boy's voice at his elbow.

Wentworth paused in his brisk stride, turned to gaze into Arthur Merriwell's forthright eyes.

"I heard what you told father," he said swiftly, a slight embarrassment flushing his cheeks at the confession of eavesdropping, "and I think your suspicions of Cartwright stealing from father are entirely correct. As to the rest of it, I can only guess. But you mentioned those murders in which Caro—Miss Davis has been foolishly involved by the police."

Wentworth regarded the boy fixedly. There was good stuff in him. The square built jaw, the firm mouth confirmed the candor and courage of the eyes.

"What do you want to know about Caroline Davis?" Wentworth asked quietly.

The boy sucked in his breath. "You do know something!" he said tensely. "Caroline disappeared, and I haven't heard a word…."

"Caroline is safe," Wentworth said kindly. "She will be safer if she does not communicate with you for the present."

The boy flushed again, looked down at the floor, then raised his gaze to meet Wentworth's.

"If you are helping Caroline," he said, "I'll help you in any way I can, any way at all."

Wentworth smiled slightly. "Just now," he said, "I'm interested in having a little talk with Sidney Cartwright. His office never knows where to find him, apparently, and…."

"Cartwright is going to see me box tonight," Arthur Merriwell replied quickly. "I'm an amateur and we're putting on a bout up at Hayes' place tonight. I think you could see him there all right!"

"Hayes?" Wentworth murmured. "Ah, yes. That will be an invitation affair. If you can let me have a card, that will do very nicely."

The boy fumbled in his wallet, gave Wentworth the card he asked. Then they shook hands and parted. The Spider was smiling as he sped back toward the city. Merriwell had not consented to help, but Wentworth had a friend in the house and it was possible that, at a later date, he might win the old man's millions as an ally. Especially after the Spider had his little talk with Cartwright tonight.

WENTWORTH KNEW Hayes' gymnasium well. Gentleman Jack Hayes he had been in pugilistic days—for Hayes was a notable fencing master and there was not a *maitre* in the city but had on at least one occasion faced the flashing steel of Wentworth's foil. At the entrance of that gymnasium then, shortly before nine o'clock, Wentworth presented himself. He was immaculate in tuxedo and chesterfield, a swagger goldheaded cane in his gloved hand. His eyes were vacuous behind a monocle, his hair curly and blond when he uncovered it in the softly lighted foyer. He checked hat and coat, left the foyer for the high shadows of the main gymnasium floor.

The floor was in darkness save for the raised brilliant square of the ring where two flyweights weaved and skipped about each other. Wentworth's eyes skimmed over the half-concealed audience. Somewhere here was Cartwright.

The flyweights finished the bout with a thwacking exchange in the middle of the ring, the lights flared briefly and the announcer climbed through the ropes. Wentworth saw that it was Gentleman Jack himself, as suave as any of the patrons in his formal black and white. He raised long-fingered hands above the pomaded glisten of his black hair, and sibilant whispers dwindled into silence.

With a shouting utterance that would have done credit to Joe Humphries of Madison Square Garden fame, he announced the winner. The fighters danced across to shake hands, and their successors clambered into the ring. One of them was Arthur Merriwell. Wentworth smiled as he shucked off his robe and bounced on the ropes in his corner. The youth was smoothly muscled and well built.

Wentworth watched three rounds of a fast bout; then, as the bell clanged for the final, he made his way back of the tiers of seats toward the dressing rooms and the showers. He was familiar with the floor plan of the gymnasium.

It was the work of moments to locate the dressing room that had been assigned to Merriwell. To reach the place, it was necessary to pass the entrance to the shower-room. It was empty, for those who were here tonight would use private baths. Wentworth stepped in there a moment and twisted a handle. Water poured on the tile floor and steam arose in folding clouds. He nodded and strolled on to Merriwell's room, entered with a knock.

A slope-shouldered man in white ducks and an athletic shirt hopped down off a rubdown table.

"I just want to wait for good old Merriwell," said Wentworth, grinning emptily. "He's putting up a capital fight, but I'm afraid the other chappie is a bit too experienced for him."

The slope-shouldered one jerked a nod, and eased back to his seat. In less than five minutes, young Merriwell came in and flopped on the rub-down table.

"You didn't fight worth a damn," a friend was scoffing at him. "You should have put him away in the second."

"But, Bill," Merriwell protested. "You know damned well I'm so worried about Caroline...."

He broke off to nod pleasantly as Wentworth walked up with effusive congratulations, unrecognizable in his disguises. Then Wentworth strolled out. The boy would think they had met somewhere before, and the Spider had done what he wanted— merely to issue from the boy's dressing room after his entrance. He was anxious not to involve young Merriwell. He stepped hurriedly from the door.

"I say there," he called to an attendant. "Find Sidney Cartwright and tell him young Merriwell wants to see him right away. He says it's damnably important."

The uniformed boy hurried away after a glance at the tip. Wentworth strolled slowly after him, stood waiting at the door which gave entrance to the main hall.

Wentworth drove the thoughts from his mind.

In moments now, Cartwright should come through the doorway in answer to the summons. After that the play must be fast and deft or an alarm would be given—and for the Spider an alarm might well mean death.

WENTWORTH CURSED softly as he saw the lawyer's erect, swagger-shouldered figure rise against the lights of the ring. The uniformed attendant strode briskly away in the opposite direction, but Cartwright was not coming alone! Two rows of seats behind him, another man whose chunky alert body fairly shouted that he was from the police, got to his feet and strolled behind the lawyer. Of course he would be guarded. Wasn't he a witness against the Spider?

The hard smile twisted the Spider's lips again as he saw his slim odds further reduced, but he drove the grimace away, made his face vacuous and adenoidal. Cartwright stepped into the dim corridor with the guard not two paces behind.

Wentworth moved quietly from the shadows. "I say, old deah," he drawled. "Young Merriwell asked me to bring you to him. I'm Reggie Montague."

Cartwright glanced sharply at Wentworth. The police guard stopped and glared, his head thrust forward.

"Right up this way," Wentworth waved a hand vaguely. "I say, that Johnnie fighting young Merriwell was quite a scrapper, eh, what?" He ambled beside the erect-shouldered lawyer—was conscious of the trailing guard.

"Merriwell said it was important, did he?"

Cartwright asked slowly. "Do you know what he wants?"

"He did mention a girl named Caroline," Wentworth chuckled.

Watching narrowly, he could have sworn that a start jerked at the face muscles of the wary lawyer. The man's face remained impassive.

"He's probably in trouble with some girl," he said calmly.

"Probably," Wentworth agreed. "I say, what's this blighter following us for?" He turned to confront the police detective. "Run along, my man," he said loftily. "We have no need...."

"Put up your hands, Mr. *Montague,*" Cartwright said sharply. His pronunciation of the name was a sneer. "Peters, see if he has a gun."

Wentworth let his mouth gape, his monocle drop from his eye as he turned toward Cartwright. The lawyer had an automatic in his hand, held it close against Wentworth's side.

"Arthur Merriwell has no friends called Montague," Cartwright snarled. "Also, he is known to most people as Arthur Ryder. Therefore, we'll just look you over a bit, Mr. *Montague!*"

Wentworth spluttered protests. It was an outrage, he declared. He would have the law upon them. But Wentworth's empty-seeing eyes were swiftly surveying the situation. Peters, the police guard, had dragged out a long-barreled thirty-eight and had leveled it carelessly. He was grinning.

"That's sweet work, Mr. Cartwright," he complimented the lawyer.

Wentworth could not submit to search for that would reveal his disguise. Revelation of his identity would land him hopelessly behind prison doors, would leave this man and his cohorts free to work their havoc on the people.

Peters came forward alertly. "I'll just frisk him, Mr. Cartwright," he said with a chuckle. "Looks like you were right in figuring the Spider would make a try for you after you accused him."

What the devil! Had Cartwright deliberately set a trap for the Spider? Wentworth glanced down the hall. Three men were walking hurriedly toward them; all had the right hands in their coat pockets. No way of knowing whether those three were police or gangsters, but guns would be useless here anyway. A single shot would trap him hopelessly by throwing the entire force of workers, the entire crowd between him and the exits! God alone knew how many of his killers Cartwright had assembled here....

He turned back to face Peters and the gloating lawyer. "Okay, Cartwright," Wentworth drawled. "I guess you got me."

CHAPTER 6
A CORPSE JUMPS

CARTWRIGHT LET out a sharp laugh at Wentworth's apparent surrender. "Got you!" he said viciously. "I'll tell the world we've got you!"

He reached out his automatic to dig its muzzle into his prisoner's ribs. The Spider winced away. As his body swayed, he jerked up his knee against Cartwright's wrist. His left darted out and the knuckles caught Peters flush on the point of the jaw.

A shout rang down the corridor. The three men had spotted his break for liberty.

Wentworth did not turn his head toward them, nor did he strike Peters again. It wasn't necessary. The chunky detective reeled back under the blow, wavered and went down hard. Before he hit the floor, Wentworth was springing on Cartwright. That blow with his knee had only knocked aside the automatic and numbed the lawyer's wrist. Now Wentworth struck again with his fist and the weapon thudded to the floor. His arms flew about Cartwright, pinning down his arms, and he yanked him clear of the floor, whirled to face the three on-racing men.

They were twenty feet away and lights glinted on guns in their hands. The door to the shower room was less than ten feet distant. Wentworth sprang toward it, carrying the writhing, fighting lawyer with him. The man was powerful; corded muscles swelled against the imprisoning arms, but the Spider's grip was like steel. He wrestled Cartwright through the doorway. Instantly he freed the man, whipped across a left that laid him unconscious on the floor. He spun toward the corridor. His hand gripped his deadly air-pistol.

With a vicious *ping*, a tiny pellet sped through the half-dark of the hall. One of the charging men cried out and dropped his weapon. He nursed his gun hand and shrank back while the other two charged on. Wentworth stung their feet with swift lead.

"I'd advise you to stay right there," Wentworth called softly. "Or I shall be compelled to shoot at your heads."

By way of emphasis, he sent another pellet winging toward

"A warning to you!" he called. "Here is what happens to those who oppose the Spider!"

them. It nipped the lobe of a mans ear. The fellow paused, cursing with rage, and raised his gun.

"Your bullets will only kill Cartwright," Wentworth admonished. "I'm behind him."

The men hesitated and Wentworth eased back from the doorway. He could see the men were cowed, that he need not worry about them for a few seconds and seconds were incredibly precious. He crouched over the curly-headed lawyer and slapped his face heavily until Cartwright regained consciousness, then dragged him toward the shower that a half-hour before he had turned on.

Steam from the hissing jets of water had clouded the cubicle like a Turkish bath. Wentworth yanked the lawyer to his feet, pinned him against the narrow opening.

"Cartwright," said Wentworth softly. "Either you talk, or I'll knock you out and toss you under that shower. It's quite warm, as you perceive. In two minutes, or less, it would scald all the skin from your body. You would die—but not immediately, of course."

A hoarse sound formed in Cartwright's throat. It was not a word, not a cry. It was the inarticulate protest of his soul against the horror of death by the torture of steam.

Glancing over his shoulder, Wentworth saw that the three men had gone, undoubtedly for reinforcements. He shoved Cartwright toward the shower so that the torrid clouds of steam swirled their humid breath into his face.

"I have no time to argue," Wentworth snapped. "Either you talk at once, or you'll die. And I'll get the information somewhere else."

"You wouldn't… wouldn't…!"

CARTWRIGHT WAS mad with fear. His smoothly corded muscles were trembling in terror. He began to battle frenziedly, but a light chopping blow behind his ear took the fight out of him.

"I'll count three," Wentworth grated harshly. "And Heaven help you if you hesitate. Fool! The Spider has you in his power!"

Wentworth threw another look over his shoulder.

"One!" he said.

Was that a man's shadow that moved by the doorway? He snapped an over-shoulder shot to clip wood from the jamb. The shadow flinched back. Wentworth nodded. They would risk nothing desperate. They figured it wouldn't be necessary with the Spider trapped in a room that had no exits, with ample reinforcements within easy reach.

"Two!" Wentworth snarled in Cartwright's ear.

He tightened his grip on the man's collar, urged him further into the shower room. A wild jet of the steaming water touched his trouser leg and the burn of it ate through.

Cartwright screeched shrilly: "I'll talk! I'll talk!" Wentworth hauled him back from the shower.

"Where are your headquarters?" he snapped. "Who are your partners?"

Cartwright twisted his frightened face about. A stray beam of light filtered through the doorway and fell upon it, showed his horrid fear. "I'll tell anything" he babbled. "Only don't throw me in that shower." The man was almost out of his head with terror.

A frown contorted Wentworth's forehead. No man so cowardly, so weak could have planned and executed the crimes of which he reaped the benefits. There were others above Cartwright, and... The movement of a shadow in the hall jerked Wentworth's head that way. A hand with a gun thrust out of a doorway across the corridor.

Wentworth flung himself backward in frantic haste as flame blossomed at the gun muzzle. The crash of the shot was echoed by another fearsome sound. The wet thud of a bullet hitting flesh, the scream of a man wounded unto death!

With a snarl, Wentworth spun toward Cartwright.

The lawyer's head was jerked far back on his shoulders, his wide eyes were staring straight upward. Abruptly, the starch went out of the man's joints and he collapsed to the floor. No need to examine him for signs of life, no need to attempt to drag him from this trap for questioning. Cartwright would never speak again.

That shot brought to Wentworth the realization that in his moment's insight into Cartwright's true nature, he had struck upon the truth. Cartwright was only a figurehead. The real villain was some other, more powerful man. And that mouth-shutting shot had sped at the Master Villain's bidding. He feared that the Spider, even trapped as he was with a dozen guns waiting for him outside the door, might escape and use those secrets.

Wentworth was sure that the hidden killer had planned a second shot to dispose also of the Spider, but reckoned that safety lay in first closing his underling's mouth. It was in character with the other ultra-careful plannings of this Torture Killer, planning that allowed for three, even four failures of his perfect organization, and even then was shaped to snatch victory from defeat.

But there was no time to speculate upon the Master now. The tense low calls in the corridor, the whisper of many feet told him that the forces of death were closing in on him, had him penned

86

in a prison that had only a single opening—and that guarded by a dozen ready guns! Here was a spot from which the Spider could not fight his way. But he had other weapons than guns. His hands moved swiftly to the kit he always carried beneath his arm, the kit that contained disguise make-up and a few simple tools that were indispensable in his work.

HE MADE a swift loop in a length of his famous silken rope, dragged Cartwright's body from the path of light at the door. Then he went to work on his own face. He had not anticipated this situation precisely, but he had thought it possible that he might have to pass himself off as Cartwright in making an escape, so the wig he wore was curly and blond and his forehead was high and peaked like the dead lawyer's. It was the work of moments to coat his pallid face with sun-tan grease-paint, to sprawl crimson lines like blood from a wound-like spot upon his forehead—and to affix beside it a paper Spider seal in imitation of the tattoo he carried in his cigarette lighter.

Then he crept toward the door, climbed upon a bench there. "A warning to you!" he called mockingly. "Here is what happens to those who oppose the Spider!"

He flung himself through the doorway, but not as a man leaps. He went with arms and legs dangling limply as if he had been a corpse caught up by trousers' seat and collar and tossed out of the way. As he hurtled through the air, he allowed his body to twist, his back to flex so that he landed on his knees, then pitched forward on his face. His forehead struck the floor heavily and he slopped over on his back with pain throbbing through his head.

The blow had hurt like the devil, but he dared not wince, dared not show pain. What pain could a corpse suffer? Through stiff unmoving lips, Wentworth sent mocking laughter—laughter from deep within his chest as a ventriloquist talks.

"Take warning," he whispered piercingly. "Make way for the Spider!"

Gasps of horror filled the hall. All eyes were fixed on the prostrate form that seemed to be the corpse of Sidney Cartwright with the red seal of the Spider on its forehead. For a moment, the men stared at him, then their gazes swung back to the black doorway from which Death had issued. At a tense order, the ten men grouped in the hall moved fearfully toward that doorway—and Wentworth watched from beneath lowered lids. When they rushed, when all attention was turned from him, he hoped to slip into the shadows and escape. A headache, a swollen nose would be a cheap price to pay for liberty.

His whole face seemed numb from the blow of striking the floor. Abruptly, Wentworth went cold with fear. Sensation was returning to his nose, and within his nostrils he could feel the slow trickle of blood. His fall had made his nose bleed—and corpses do not bleed!

If there was among these ten men one who had half the sense of their leader, if the leader himself still were hidden in that dark doorway whence the gun had vomited death, he would know how to deal with bleeding corpses. A second shot placed beside that dummy wound upon his forehead would settle all doubts.

Desperately, Wentworth's heavy-lidded eyes kept watch. He could do nothing to halt the flow of blood. If only it did not bleed too much, he might escape. A man shot through the head might well have such a hemorrhage, but it would be sluggish and would cease almost immediately. He lolled his eyes toward that doorway from which the gun that killed Cartwright had jutted—and tension almost jerked him to his feet.

The gun was thrust from the doorway again—and *its muzzle was aimed at Wentworth's heart!*

SWIFT AS light, Wentworth's eyes flicked to the other men in the hall. None of them was looking at him. For seconds, he would be free of that danger, free to face the greater peril of that leveled, terribly-accurate gun in the dark. With no preliminary tensing of muscles, Wentworth rolled. He twitched to the left and his right hand raked to the automatic beneath his arm as he moved.

The gun in the doorway spat and Wentworth felt the burn of lead, the shock of a bullet against his ribs. He had his own automatic now and its flame lanced toward that thin deadly hand. He was moving even as he fired, was up on his knees and plunging to the safety of the wall beside the door.

The killer's gun did not speak again, although Wentworth knew his shot had been too hurried to have hit the man. It was as if that hidden monster did not fire except to kill, as if he scorned to waste lead that could only frighten—that would not find a human wound in which to rest. The Spider was safe for the moment from that weapon, but ten other men in the hall were whirling now, whirling with ready guns.

Wentworth's disguise as a corpse still fought for him. The sight of a dead man on his feet despite a bullet hole through his forehead would have unnerved more intelligent men than these strong-arm killers. Furthermore, they sought the Spider; they had no quarrel with the corpse of Sidney Cartwright.

Wentworth did not make the mistake of a frantic dash for escape. Stiff-legged, staring-eyed as a sleep-walker, he stalked toward the nearest of the killers—and took care that the lurking monster in that darkened doorway had no chance to put a bullet in his back.

A violent tremor shook the gunman toward whom he stalked. The man's arms went lax and his gun dropped to the floor. Muscles jerked in his legs. He wanted to run, but fear had paralyzed him. His mouth opened and closed twice, soundlessly. The third time, a scream came tearing forth. As if that had broken the spell, he whirled and pounded down the hall—toward a doorway into the main hall. Hoarse cries continued to rip from him. He plunged into the doorway and smacked into a solid rank of men in evening dress. They tangled, fighting and cursing.

Wentworth realized, then, that the shots had been the first warning to the Hayes guests of the grim tragedy that was being enacted within yards of where they sat. He did not pause in his stiff-legged stride, but stalked straight toward the bunched men, the blood and the Spider seal on his face.

Shocked horror stopped the rush of men, but they formed a solid rank across his path. Wentworth marched on as if they had not been there. What would he do if they failed to open a path for him? A touch of his hand, a close glimpse of that hurriedly faked wound on his forehead and someone would detect the fraud. Furthermore, these men had not seen an apparent corpse rise and walk. Their shock would not be so great. Their intelligence would penetrate the deception.

The fleeing strong-arm man clawed frantically as he fought to put more space between himself and this walking corpse with its fixed eyes. Wentworth paced on. He was within three feet of the close-packed ranks now. Behind him came a sudden shout.

"Stop him!" cried a deep voice. "Cartwright's body is in here. *That man is the Spider!*" The words boomed in the sudden stillness of the corridor. *"The Spider!"* reverberated through the building.

On their heels, guns thundered and lead screamed toward the hallway where Wentworth fled. Men cried out as the wild bullets dug into their vitals. Once more the killers, callous of human life, were slaughtering crazily in a mad effort to get the Spider. Wentworth saw four men go down under the fire. He whirled and poured a clip of bullets into the midst of the killer's charge. Police would not fire like that when their shots might strike down innocents. They would rather have the Spider escape.

WENTWORTH SAW three gangsters wilt before his fire, then he whirled to flee. The crowd melted away from before him. The shots and the cry of Spider had electrified the men, but instead of plunging to halt this stalking corpse-man with a gun in his hand, they turned and ran. And for once Wentworth was glad that his name struck terror to men's hearts. Still, he was unhurried as he pivoted into the doorway whence all had fled.

"The Spider! The Spider!" men shouted as they ran. The entire building echoed with the cry. The place was in turmoil. Two men clad only in trunks stood with hanging arms in the ring.

The referee stared between them at the rout in the dimness beyond the white canvas. Then abruptly, he, too, fled. He hand vaulted the ropes, plunged into the midst of the panic. Chairs were overturned with a rending crash of broken wood. Men struck out frantically with their fists as the mad mob spirit of fear seized them.

Wentworth snapped out of his slow-paced flight, sprinted to join the ranks of those who fled from him. He pressed his forehead into the crook of his elbow as if he feared to look behind him—it hid the seal and fake wound—and fought as wildly as any other to escape.

"The Spider! The Spider!" Wentworth howled.

"Don't let the Spider get me!"

His shout helped spread panic and the outer doors of the hall burst with explosive violence beneath the pressure of fighting men. In the midst of the panic-stricken mob, Wentworth was swept out into the street. Forehead still buried in the crook of his elbow, he darted for the shadows. A figure materialized from the darkness and a straight-armed hand caught him on the chest.

"Hold on, buddy," a man growled.

Wentworth jerked down his arm, revealing the gory forehead, the seal of the Spider. The man gasped, reeled back and went down beneath Wentworth's swift blow. The punch was hurried, though, and as the Spider raced on, he heard the man shout wildly, heard his pounding feet take up the pursuit. A gun blasted behind and lead whined past Wentworth's ears. This man must be one of those who had found Cartwright's body.

He must have used some hidden exit from the building, circled to trap the fugitive.

Then Gentleman Jack Hayes was party to the conspiracy also! He and his gymnasium attendants must be tied up with Cartwright in some way! Dodging from side to side as he raced for cover, Wentworth recognized the truth of that surmise at once. He should have seen that long ago when so many bravos—palpably not from the police—had rallied to snatch Cartwright from danger, from the possibility of squealing.

Wentworth was streaking along a half-darkened street now. A hundred feet ahead, a street lamp pooled white light on the pavement. On either side were the gaunt doorways of tenements interspersed with warehouses. He could look for no succor here, nor could he hope that crowds would frighten off pursuit. He could tell by the shouting behind him that others had joined in the chase. No longer was there any question of dropping a single criminal and thus escaping. Now he must defeat an entire pack of wolves. And among them might well be police and innocent parties at whom the Spider could not strike.

Bullets sang like hornets about his head.

Wentworth was suddenly aware of a stabbing pain in his side. He recalled with a sense of shock that the hidden marksman of the darkened doorway had scored there with his lead. He pressed a hand against his ribs, felt the warm stickiness of blood. The wound could not be serious, or he would never have risen from the floor but the hemorrhage was sapping his strength. His breath was corning in gulps. There was a heaviness in his legs instead of his usual bounding strength.

Gasping, Wentworth snatched at the brick facing of a doorway as he bolted past, whirled himself into the opening. He caromed off a wall, stumbled over the door-step and was bounding up shaking stairs in great striding leaps. It was his last gasp of
strength. He reached the top floor, hurled himself prone, gun in hand. He could not fire to hit police, if any were in that polyglot mob at his heels, but bullets smacking into the wall above their heads should hold them in check, until, until—

Blankly, Wentworth asked himself—until what? His strength was spent. Death was closing in on him in a form he could not fight effectively, death at the hands of the police he had assisted so ably. That they would be fighting, side by side, with killers and crooks did not alter his position. Probably, with their usual wily strategy, the criminals would retire now that they had holed up the Spider and let the forces of law and order drag him out for the kill.

BELOW HIM, Wentworth could hear the frightened jabbering of the tenants of the house. A slight smile twisted his lips. If the police were taking over the chase, they would clear the house of people before they began a serious attack. At least, he would have a breathing space. Perhaps he would be able to find a way over the roofs. But he shook his head even as he thought that. This house, the entire block, would already be surrounded.

Then Wentworth sprang to his feet with a strangled shout. A muffled plop had sounded in the hall near him, the explosion of a gas-bomb detonator. Even as he reeled up, acrid fumes stabbed pain into his eyes. He darted down the hall, then staggered back, peering blearily through tears and ache. Red tongues of flame leaped upward in his path. He whirled, stared back the other way. Fire blazed there, too.

They had run the Spider to earth at last, blinded him, set fire to his last retreat—and outside, cruel, deadly guns awaited him. Mounting light flickered through the hall now. Overhead a gun blasted, lead thudded into the floor at his feet. Wentworth's automatic spat an answer and a man screamed; a black form pitched downward into the path of the flames.

Wentworth flung back his head and laughed. It was rasping, despairing laughter. Through his streaming, aching eyes, he could just make out the body that lay in the hall. His shot had been guided home by the instinct of long practice.

Still sobbing with horrible laughter, the Spider wrenched his victim over on his back, planted upon his brows the red seal of the Spider. They might pull down the Spider, might run him to earth at last, but he would not go from the battle alone. Staggering with the effort, Wentworth lifted the body at arm's length above his head, hurled it across flame and boiling smoke, sent it smashing through a window and hurtling downward into the street.

"Come on!" he shrieked. "Come on! The Spider still has his fangs!"

CHAPTER 7
EYES THAT SEE NOT

THAT SHRIEK of defiance snapped the mad tension that had gripped him. Abruptly as it had risen, his fury died and was supplanted by a cold determination to survive—to wipe out these killers, to run to earth the criminal genius who headed them. He peered upward blindly at the spot from which the shot had come. Dimly, he made out an opening. Even as he spotted it, he shook his head. That was futile. If one man had found his way there to toss that gas bomb, others might well follow to mete out death.

From below came the screams of frightened people. Even through the blur of the pain that tore at throat and nostrils and eyes, Wentworth could distinguish their terror. The song of the flames had risen to a bellowing roar. Heat pressed in upon him from behind, from in front. Dense smoke whirled about him. He shook his head violently, swabbed at his eyes with his sleeve.

The flapping light of the fire seemed not to reach to the left wall, but he could not be sure. His eyes, streaming with tears, were nearly useless. Still it was his only chance, to squeeze past that fearsome barrier and strive to find a safe way to the street. Already, a vague plan was forming in his fertile brain....

He ripped his coat from his shoulders, bundled it over his head and sprang forward along the left wall. For a moment, intolerable heat scorched him, then the floor opened under his feet and he pitched downward. With a frantic effort he caught himself. He had jumped on the stairs and now the heat was above him. Desperately, Wentworth scrambled on. Here all was soft velvety blackness before his tortured eyes. The light of the flames above could not lift that curtain for him.

He brought up with a staggering blow against a wall. For a moment panic tugged at his heart. What chance did a blind man have against such enemies? He recalled abruptly that, contrary to the usual tear gas whose effects fade in from twenty minutes to an hour, the previous attack upon him had blurred his vision for hours. He had never fully recovered from it and this second attack, in addition to the excruciating pain, had robbed him of all sight. The fiends were using some powerful acid gas! Good Lord in heaven, suppose—suppose these two gassings should blind him permanently!

Wentworth fought down the fear frantically. He must, above all things, remain calm. A terrified man cannot escape calm enemies. He twisted his blind face toward the upward stairs. It seemed to him that the glare was hotter, the light greater. He must hurry....

Wentworth dug into his kit again, swabbed off the grease-paint of his disguise; he wiped off, too, the false wound and the paper seal of the Spider that he had put upon his forehead. He hurled the blond wig above him toward the fire. After it he tossed his coat and formal shirt. Then, stripped to his under-shirt, he groped along the hall. A door flung open in his path and he staggered back, snatching for his gun. Hands gripped his thighs, but they were tiny hands. It was the voice of a terrified child that cried up to him.

97

"I'm afraid!" it sobbed.

Wentworth stood stock-still with the baby hands clutching at his legs. He dropped his gun into its holster, groped and found a head of curly hair that did not reach to his waist.

"I'm afraid," the child sobbed again. "And muvver won't get up."

Something like a sob rose into Wentworth's own throat; his mouth twisted in a grin of self mockery. The escape of the Spider did not include carrying a helpless baby and its mother to safety, for it was apparent that the child's mother had been overcome in her room. The Spider had planned to grope secretly into the darkness of the basement to hide himself there, hoping that the firemen would overcome the flames and permit him finally to win his way to freedom. Alone, he might accomplish that, but not with a child and a helpless woman. Besides, the woman probably would die if she did not obtain prompt medical treatment. Being overcome by smoke puts poison into the system— poison that works fearfully upon the tissues.

Well, he had sacrificed the people he loved to the ideal of justice before, hadn't he? Many times he had defeated criminals who sought to force his compliance with their foul plans by threatening death to his darling Nita. He had defeated them by ignoring their threats, by choosing that Nita should die. In the end, he had always managed to save her, but that had been mere chance. His sacrifice was just as painful.

WHY, THEN, shouldn't the Spider sacrifice these two people so that in the end he might wipe out this fearful threat to humanity, these beasts who slew mercilessly, who would not hesitate to burn a house filled with living souls for their own selfish ends? Wentworth knew that the fire trap had been set in this house long before he had stumbled upon it.

He knew that the crooks had intended to burn the building for some part of their commercial conspiracy. He had stumbled into it and they had immediately availed themselves of their preparations to rid themselves of the Spider. He knew these things because it would have been impossible for any man to have started the fires on each side of him as it had been done, except through some fire-trap that had been rigged in advance.

Thousands more undoubtedly would die if these criminals continued their work. Would it not be better to sacrifice these two—mother and child—in order that the Spider might survive to battle?

Wentworth's mind said that it would, but the sardonic grin had not left his mouth and even as he mocked himself, he stooped, and groping, found the child's face with his fingers.

"Don't be afraid, child," he said softly. "Take me to your mother."

He took the baby's pudgy hand in his own, followed blindly where it tugged. The heat about him increased steadily. The smoke was fiery torture to lungs and eyes. The child was coughing, beginning to cry.

"I'm afraid," it whimpered.

"Where is your mother?" Wentworth asked.

He took a half-step hesitantly and his knee caught on the yielding side of a bed. He groped with one hand and found the body of a woman.

Wentworth clamped his jaws, and forced himself to pay out the line slowly.

"Hold on to my leg," he told the child. "And don't let go for anything."

"I'm afraid… *afraid.*"

The child clung with both chubby hands.

Wentworth lifted the woman awkwardly to his shoulder. He reeled beneath the burden, though it was light, then took the child's hand.

"I can't see," he said. "Lead me to the steps, baby, the steps going down."

His lips were still twisted thinly. Where were the firemen, he wondered, that they had failed to find these two? He stepped out hesitantly, guiding himself by the tugging of the child's hand; then he heard the baby sob, felt the tiny body cower against his legs.

"Ooooh," the child moaned. "Fire burns!" Wentworth could feel intolerable heat upon his own face, and he shrank back, too. He knew now why the firemen had not come. The fiends who had set this building afire had not been content to ignite it on the top floor. They had started flames below also. The way of escape was blocked!

Fumes bit into his lungs and raked him with coughing. He staggered under the burden of the woman and his hand flinched from the touch of a wall that seemed red hot. He pulled the child back.

"The window?" he gasped between coughs.

"Take me to the window!"

Thank God, he still carried his Spider kit with its powerful silken line strapped beneath his arm. The struggle to the window was endless, but finally the gushing draft of smoke and hot air about him told that it was near. Wentworth ripped off kit and gun holster, tossed them behind him toward the advancing flames. Swiftly he climbed out of the incriminating dress trousers he still wore, used them to wrap the silken cord before he knotted it beneath the woman's arms.

Then he twisted the line about his body and forearms and, lifting the woman over the sill, paid it out slowly. The child pressing against his leg began to sob again between tearing coughs. Wentworth himself was shaken by the bite of the fumes in his lungs. His eyes were balls of fire. He clamped his teeth, forced himself to payout the line slowly. He must do that since he could not see the ground. The silk bit into his hands.

Finally the line slacked and he knew the woman's body had reached the earth. He knotted the silk about the sash hurriedly, looped it over both upper and lower windows for greater strength. Then catching the child up, he straddled the sill. It was the work of moments to twist the line about his arms and legs. Then he slipped off into space. Heat billowed and sucked about him. The child sobbed. Shouts came from below.

"Hurry! Hurry!" a man cried. "The line is burning!"

WENTWORTH PEERED downward blindly, loosened the silk and let it speed about his arms and thighs. He could feel the give of the line as the flame licked at it, high above. Then abruptly, the restraint was gone—he was falling, falling. He twisted, cushioned the child on his chest, hit the earth heavily, almost flat on his back.

Luckily, the fall had been short. Though it drove the breath from his body and dazed him. As it was he did not lose consciousness. He felt the child snatched to safety, felt friendly hands upon his arms as he, too, was carried from the overhanging threat of the doomed building. He stumbled as he walked.

"What's the matter, buddy?" a man grumbled.

"Can't you see where you're going?"

"I'm afraid not," Wentworth said, his mouth twisting wryly. "Smoke gets in your eyes."

The man cursed. "Anybody that can joke when people are dying…" he mumbled.

His hand jerked away from Wentworth's arm and the Spider stood still. He could hear bustle and movement about him, hear the whimpering of a child's small voice. He could hear the crackle and roar of the fire, the shouts of men and the trample of their feet. The smell of the smoke and the cutting clean pungency of antiseptics reached his nostrils.

"Where is the ambulance?" Wentworth asked in a normal tone of voice. He could not tell whether or not anyone was near him. An enemy with his gun out might stand at his elbow. There might not be anyone nearer than fifty feet. He started as a hand touched his arm.

"The ambulance is over here," a man's voice said at his elbow. "Come this way." Wentworth followed where the man led, but tension rippled through his muscles. He knew his enemies were all about him—that scent of antiseptics was growing dimmer instead of stronger. He stopped in his tracks, in an agony of indecision.

"Over this way," the voice said urgently. "Hurry, I have other cases to attend to."

"Never mind," Wentworth said. "Take care of the others."

"I can't leave you like this," the man insisted. His fingers clenched more tightly about Wentworth's arm. He tugged still farther away from the clean scent of the antiseptics that meant safety.

Wentworth jerked clear of the man's grip, swung his fist in a looping wild blow. It found flesh and the man grunted. Wentworth spun and ran back the way he had come. He dodged from side to side, bent far forward. Never in Wentworth's adventurous life had he done a thing that required so much courage as running blindly. Any footfall might plunge him into a pit. He might be charging head foremost into a brick wall. He might be plunging straight into the arms of the killers.

Directly ahead of him a man shouted. "Hey, watch out there!"

Wentworth checked, straightened, his chest panting, his blind face peering.

"Trying to kill my patients, you fool?" the man demanded irascibly.

Wentworth gulped with relief. "Are you the interne?" he asked swiftly.

The man grumbled assent. Wentworth sank to the ground. "I'm blind," he said simply. "When you can spare the time, will you get a policeman to help me?"

A man spoke behind him. "He's not only blind, he's out of his head, mister. I'm his friend and he won't let me help him."

Wentworth crouched without moving. He did not know that

105

voice, but he knew it meant death. It was undoubtedly one of the killers. He must either trust himself to this man, or turn to the police and hope against hope that he would not be recognized. And he could not see. He could not see… What chance did a blind Spider have?

THE INTERNE cursed impatiently. "Good God, isn't all this bad enough without dumping a crazy man on my hands?"

Wentworth let his left hand trail on the ground, searching for some weapon he could use in emergency. Evidently, the situation was such that the enemy did not dare to kill him here—preferred to inveigle him away.

"I don't know you," Wentworth said shortly.

"I'm not crazy. I prefer to place myself in a policeman's hands. Doctor, you must help me."

His voice was not that of the usual tenement dweller and this fact apparently penetrated the interne's irritation. Wentworth heard quick footsteps approach.

"Listen," the interne said sharply. "If the man wants to stay here, why not leave him here? You've got to humor crazy men you know. Get a policeman if you like. Now get away and let me do my work."

The man Wentworth was sure was one of the killers protested, but the interne cut him short with another order to get away.

"I'll get a policeman," the man threatened. "Then get him," the interne swore. "Your crazy man says he'll go with a cop."

Wentworth listened with an impassive face to this argument above him. It was as if he were an inanimate object of great value over which men fought. Well—his mouth twisted wryly—he wasn't of much more value than so much mud squatting here like *this*. There was no telling how long this blindness might continue. The pain in his eyes was still fearful….

"That's the man there, muvver," the child's voice broke in on his thoughts. He turned his sightless eyes toward the sound of the voice.

"That's the man," the child said again.

Hope bounded up within Wentworth. He straightened, strained his eyes futilely.

"You saved me and Florence!" A woman spoke so close to him that Wentworth started. "You saved me and my little girl!"

"Hey!" the interne shouted. "What the hell is this?"

"It's quite all right," Wentworth assured him swiftly. "I carried this lady and her child out of the building and she's offered to help me."

"Oh, if I only could…" the woman said eagerly.

The interne broke into blasphemous cursing. "Then for God's sake get out of here and quit bothering me!"

"Quickly," Wentworth whispered. "Take me away to a dark spot where I can't be seen. There are men here who want to kill me."

The woman's breath sucked in quickly. But death often stalks in the tenements. She did not doubt. Her hand met Wentworth's groping fingers and together they moved slowly away. From time to time the woman coughed painfully. Their feet shuffled and in the distance men shouted. The sound of turmoil faded and at last she stopped.

"We can't be seen now," she said, whispering. "I'd like to take you to a neighbor's house, if it would be all right."

"If you could get me some clothing," Wentworth said hesitantly. His hand went to a money belt strapped beneath his underwear. He made it a point always to carry ample funds, for he never knew what emergency he might have to meet. He handed the woman a wad of bills.

"Get me some second hand clothing," he said, "an old overcoat and a pair of smoked glasses. Get me also a tin cup and a violin."

"But I can't leave you here like *this*," the woman protested.

"Where am I?"

"In an alley, between an old shed and some garbage cans," the woman explained and the scent of sour food confirmed it.

"If I crouch down can anyone see me?" Wentworth asked.

"Not unless they walk right up to you," the woman answered.

"Then leave me here," Wentworth urged, "and hurry with those things. My life depends on it."

THE WOMAN finally consented; her feet rasped away over the cobbles of the alley. The child's treble floated back and Wentworth was alone. The hour that he waited there was the longest he ever had known. His feeling of utter helplessness, his blind eyes that could make out only a distant blur of light, were a torment. Finally, the alley echoed once more, with the rasp of shoes and the piping of a child's voice and Wentworth almost shouted aloud with relief.

"There are a lot of policemen all around," the woman told him in a swift whisper. "Two of them stopped me and asked questions. I told them my father's clothes were all burned in the fire, that the violin was all we had saved and I was afraid to leave it with my father for fear it would be stolen."

Wentworth laughed softly as he rapidly donned the clothes the woman had brought him. "That was perfect," he declared. "Absolutely perfect. Now, if you happened to mention that your father was blind…."

"That was why I was afraid the violin would be stolen," she said.

Wentworth was dressed now, the smoked glasses shielding his blinded eyes, the violin case hugged under his arm. He stooped his shoulders in a semblance of age. The hesitating step of the blind was not difficult to assume. It was hard anyway to walk boldly when he could not see where the next footstep would fall. On the woman's arm, with the child clinging to his hand, they walked slowly down the dark alley and into the street. The greater noise of the traffic, the brighter rays that filtered into his blurred eyes, told Wentworth that no one challenged them.

"Where do you want to go?" the woman asked timidly.

Wentworth pressed money into her hand. "Take me to the subway nearest here," he said, "then go to a hotel."

The woman absolutely refused the money even when Wentworth protested that they were quits, that if he had saved her life, she had equally saved his. She finally told Wentworth her name and the address of friends where she'd stay and they parted at the entrance to the subway station. He would recompense her later in a way she could not refuse.

Down the steps, Wentworth groped his way and a kindly

hand assisted him on a train. For the balance of the night, he shuttled back and forth on the subway until crowds he could not see jammed the aisles and he knew the city was up and about its business again. Then he made his way to the streets. There was a constant throb and burning ache in his eyes. The pain was terrific, but that was the least of his blindness. The torture was that he could not see.

His most murderous enemy might creep upon him unbe-knownst. What hope did a blind Spider have of exterminating the Torture Killers? Of carrying the warfare to the ingenious head of the Murder Trust? Bitterly Wentworth fought down the panic that rose now and again in his breast, that stabbed him to the heart at each step that crowded too near, at each approach of men or women he could not see. He made his way with tedious caution to a post opposite the Martha Washington Hotel where Nita was keeping watch over the Davis girl, and there he began to play the violin the woman had bought for him.

It was a tiny instrument and its tenderest notes were harsh, but Wentworth's wizardry with the bow drew sweet music from its strings. He had no fear that Nita, passing, would fail to recognize him. She would know his touch upon the strings, his playing…. But hours passed and there was no sign that Nita had heard or seen. Four times he moved away from the hotel and four times returned, fearing to stay constantly lest he attract the attention of the police. He knew they were shadowing Nita, hoping again to get within striking distance of Richard Wentworth, whom all the city now believed to be a Spider gone mad.

At long last his patience was rewarded. Playing, he heard a

woman's sweet voice, a voice he knew, the voice of his darling Nita!

"Just a minute, my dear," Nita said, talking apparently to a companion, "I want to give this wonderful violinist...."

CHANGE TINKLED into the tin cup he had hooked into his worn coat pocket. Wentworth felt a tremor ripple over his body. He needed Nita so, needed her strength and her—her *eyes*. But he dared not speak. The police could stand unseen at his elbow....

"Let's call a cab," Nita went on. "I just can't wait to get to the opening of my exhibition. Probably I'll have to change prices if I expect to sell any, but here's hoping. I wish Dick could see them."

The drone of an automobile motor crescendoed, a door clicked open. The taxi was at hand. Nita gave the address of a West Fifty-Seventh street picture gallery. Wentworth's hand faltered in his playing. After all these hours of waiting, he must let Nita depart without a sign from him.

He must—must cry out to her. But he didn't.

The taxi drove off. He kept on playing for fifteen minutes before he left the stand in front of the hotel. He drove his need for Nita from his heart and mind, forced himself to think calmly. It was plain that Nita had feared to speak to him on the street, had thought or known that police were near. But she had been busy beforehand, planning a way they might communicate. He gathered that she had arranged for an exhibition of her oil paintings, a thing she never before had consented to do though noted critics had begged her to. That in itself was notable, but that she should consider price when she had independent means of support.... If Wentworth read her message right, she expected him to gain some message from her price tags. She did not know that he was blind.

He had reached a corner now, stood tapping the curbstone with his cane, waiting for some one to help him across the street. A hand touched his arm and he nodded his head in thanks and walked along with dragging feet, the cane tapping ahead, reached the other curb.

"Thank you," he said, and started to pace on slowly. But the hand continued to grip his arm. Wentworth turned a timid blank face, terror racing through his brain. Was this the enemy he had feared? Was it the police? "Did you want me to do something for you?" he asked in the passive, quiet voice of the blind. "To play something?"

"Yes," a precise, clipped voice answered. "Play me the *Devil's Trill.*"

Wentworth could have shouted aloud to hear that voice. At last, in his helplessness, he had found aid. It was Stanley Kirkpatrick, his friend! That request told him something else. The *Devil's Trill* was an unbeautiful, but technically, very difficult composition. No ordinary violinist could master its intricacies. Probably Kirkpatrick was not quite sure of his identification and wished to ascertain from his playing whether or not it was really Wentworth.

"You jest, surely, sir," Wentworth said, still in a passive tone. Then he whispered without moving his lips. "It's Dick Wentworth. I really am blind."

"No, I'm quite serious," Kirkpatrick said. "You play with

extraordinary skill. I'm sure the *Trill* is not beyond you." Then he whispered as had Wentworth. "Good God, man! Why didn't you come to me for help? Surely—" He broke off impatiently. "Come, come, I'll give you a dollar to play me the *Trill*. It's to settle a bet. A friend of mine said you couldn't do it."

"Very well, sir," Wentworth said, "I'll do my best."

He tucked his violin under his chin, but the music that issued from the instrument had lost its magic. He played horribly, with blundering fingers, but Kirkpatrick did not interrupt until he had nearly reached the end of his execrable performance. Then he whispered sharply. "Okay, Dick, come with me." His hand touched Wentworth's elbow and guided him into an automobile. "Lose that car behind," Kirkpatrick's clipped voice ordered and Wentworth felt the surging power as the motor took hold.

"Now, tell me everything," Kirkpatrick ordered and Wentworth rapidly narrated as much as he dared of what had occurred. Kirkpatrick knew he was the Spider and, for the present, he was not Police Commissioner, but there was no point in making revelations which both he and Kirkpatrick would regret. When he had finished, Kirkpatrick sat silent for a long time.

"It's obvious," Kirkpatrick said finally, "that Nita has something of importance to communicate. I'll go to the exhibition of paintings. Meantime, I'm going to have my confidential physician look at those eyes of yours. You'd better not attempt to carry on the battle until you can see again."

A SLIGHT smile touched Wentworth's lips. "If you can talk to Nita," he said. "Tell her I need Apollo."

"That Great Dane would identify you to every cop on the

street," Kirkpatrick objected sharply. "As it is, there were two cops on your trail when I picked you up—merely because Nita dropped a dime into your tin cup. You see how thoroughly Boise is doing things?"

Wentworth's sightless eyes narrowed at the name of Kirkpatrick's successor. "Had it occurred to you," he asked, "that that is the only way the Mayor could have learned of your message to me? There had to be a leak somewhere in your office. And Boise could easily have been the leak!"

"I've already thought of that, Dick. I've had private detectives on him, but they can't get anything." Kirkpatrick sounded weary. "Now that Cartwright is dead, of course there is no one to accuse me, but that does not mean I am exonerated. The Mayor even intimated that I had something to do with Cartwright's death."

Wentworth sat gazing blankly ahead of him.

"Could I listen to a radio news report?" he asked slowly.

Almost immediately the staccato voice of an announcer sounded as Kirkpatrick turned on his auto receiving set. Wentworth leaned forward, listening intently.

"... after the shooting at the gymnasium." The radio had caught the announcer in the middle of an account of the Spider's struggle at Gentleman Jack Hayes' establishment. "The Spider set fire to the building in which he was trapped and succeeded in escaping the police. Seven people were killed in the fire. When the blaze was well under way, the familiar cloaked and masked figure of the Spider was seen on top of the building. He was laughing."

Wentworth frowned. "Who saw this figure of the Spider?" he asked aloud.

"Seven policemen and at least twenty people in the street," Kirkpatrick's calm voice replied. "There can be no doubt that it appeared. I'm beginning to believe that it was seen at the scenes of other crimes, as reported."

Wentworth tightened his hands into fists that were clenched on his knees. So the Spider was to be saddled with all the crimes of the Torture Killers? They had begun with coached witnesses, but now a man who posed as the Spider actually showed himself on the scene of the crime. No longer could there be any charge of false testimony. People would swear faithfully to what they believed to be the truth.

"The hounds!" Wentworth exploded. "You know the Spider would not have set that building afire even to save himself!"

"Yes, Dick, I know that," said Kirkpatrick quietly. The words of the announcer broke in on further conversation, taking up another phase of the news.

"Congress voted today to investigate reports that inferior materials in a certain manufacturer's cars were causing a series of terrible accidents with an enormous cost of lives. One hundred and seven deaths within the last month have been blamed on breakage of vital parts...."

Wentworth beat softly upon his knees with his fists. "My God!" he cried in a smothered voice. "Do you suppose that, too, could be part of this damnable conspiracy? I know already of two of their plots: one for a building site, one for an insurance company."

Kirkpatrick did not answer and the Spider continued to listen to the announcer. He went from the account of automobile accidents to a financial item about a proxy battle for control of the Atlas Insurance Company, in which Emile Bowfee, owner of a chain of newspapers, sought to seize power. Something clicked in Wentworth's brain. It was as if, deprived of vision, his brain operated more swiftly in compensation.

"Kirk!" His exclamation was a cry. "Haven't there been more fires than usual for this time of year? Mostly in tenement districts?"

KIRKPATRICK WAS silent for a moment while Wentworth's blind face turned toward him. Finally he answered the question in the affirmative. "Now that you speak of it," he said, "there have been a great number of such fires."

"Exactly," said Wentworth. "Now here is something to find out. Were not all, or nearly all of those tenements, insured by the same company?"

"What are you getting at?" Kirkpatrick demanded. "Just this," Wentworth snapped. "After last night, I am convinced that Sidney Cartwright was only a figurehead in this vast commercial conspiracy. Some criminal brain, greater than his, ordered his execution when he was trapped last night. In escaping I ran into a fire-trap that had been rigged beforehand to destroy the tenants. I'm confident of that.

"Now then. Emile Bowfee is a client of Cartwright. He is battling for control of Atlas. You recall that Robert Kenton was an executive of Atlas. I think Kenton was killed by torture while the murderers forced information from him. I think when you

116

investigate, you'll find most of these tenements were insured by Atlas…."

Kirkpatrick broke in with an amazed curse. "You mean that Bowfee is behind these crimes!"

"I don't know," Wentworth said with tight quick words, "but you'll admit that the circumstances are suspicious. If you can check on those fires and the insuring firm—fire department records will show that—and find out whether Bowfee was party to that deal for the skyscraper site where those murders were committed, we should be able to get a very definite idea of whether he is involved."

"That sounds like a very excellent hunch," Kirkpatrick agreed slowly. "I'll look into it. My only chance of being reinstated lies in wiping out this gang and proving that you—and the Spider— are innocent of the charges. If I can do that, there no longer is any question of my helping a criminal to escape."

A smile twisted Wentworth's lips and his hand groped until it found his friend's arm. Kirkpatrick hadn't said a word about his other motives—about helping Wentworth. "I knew," he said with a laugh, "that you were only interested in helping yourself."

"I still consider it my duty to enforce the law," Kirkpatrick replied stiffly. "I only notified you of danger because I was sure it was a frame-up."

"Of course," said Wentworth, still laughing.

"Friendship doesn't enter into it."

"Oh, go to hell!" Kirkpatrick said shortly, then he laughed, too. His hand clapped Wentworth on the shoulder, and his voice was kindly as he helped the blind man from the car and led

117

him toward the doctor's office. "A damned shame we can't work together on things, Dick," he said. "Sometimes I think I ought to resign and have you appointed Commissioner of Police!"

"I think the Spider would be a much better man for the job than either one of us," Wentworth told him dryly.

THE DOCTOR went swiftly to work on Wentworth's eyes with cleansing and healing solutions, blindfolded him and ordered him to remain quiet. The treatments eased the burning pain that had persisted for days and Wentworth sat at ease, turning over in his mind the discoveries he had made in his brief and disastrous battles with the Murder Master.

His keen brain had spotted Emile Bowfee as a suspect, but the present Police Commissioner, Howard Boise, was equally in a position of doubt. Some spy, as Wentworth had told Kirkpatrick, had given out information from headquarters and Boise had been in an excellent position to betray Kirk. Cartwright undoubtedly had been a leader in the murderous gang, and it seemed likely that Gentleman Jack Hayes was party to it also. This false Spider was not necessarily the leader. He might very well be merely an underling dressed up for the part. It was all damnably clever.

Wentworth must find out what auto firm had been referred to in the radio announcer's broadcast about the congressional investigation, learn whether Bowfee—or a rival firm—was connected with that. It might be well to try once more to enlist the help of Phineas Merriwell.

Wentworth jerked up his head at the opening of the door, turning his face toward the sound. Perhaps Kirkpatrick had returned with information. No one spoke. There was no other sound except the careful closing of the door.

"Who is it?" Wentworth demanded sharply.

The intruder did not speak. Wentworth strained his ears, but could hear no sound of advance or retreat.

"Who is it?" he demanded again more sharply. This time there was an answer, soft mocking laughter that grated like a file upon Wentworth's nerves.

"I am the Spider," the man who had laughed said jeeringly. "I have come for you."

Wentworth lurched to his feet, but his speeding hand found no gun beneath his arm. He bad forgotten for the moment that he had no weapon. He stood with his fists knotted, blind face turned toward the sound of the laugh. Those damnable killers had traced him down and now the man who made sport of the Spider's name, who fastened the blame for a dozen fearful crimes upon him, had come to taunt, to kill him!

"The chief has decided," the softly mocking voice continued, "that two Spiders is one too many—and he prefers that you should be the one to resign that honor."

The keen point of a knife touched Wentworth's throat.

CHAPTER 8
NEW MURDERS

WENTWORTH STOOD rigid, feeling the prick of that knife-point at his throat. His mouth was twisted in a wry smile for he visioned himself dead with the red seal

119

of the Spider on his own forehead, exonerated in death of all the crimes with which he stood accused. But with that satiric thought came another idea: the brain of these killers would not want him murdered—yet.

If Wentworth were found dead now, with the seal on his forehead, it would prove that he was innocent of the Spider's crimes, make it necessary for a new scapegoat to be found. Wentworth had discovered one thing about the Torture Killers. Their plots demanded that there be some one to take the rap. Lately, that had been always the Spider. Obviously then, they would not kill Wentworth, whom they had identified as the Spider, until they were ready to close their books of crime.

Then this false Spider had come, not to kill, but to capture Wentworth. Swift as was his realization of that fact, his actions were more quick. That knifepoint had scarcely had time to prick his throat, before he snapped up a hand to grasp his assailant's wrist. He caught it and his right fist swept in a short, brutal arc, thudded into yielding flesh.

The knife dropped and the false Spider sprang away from that attack, his breath wheezing out beneath Wentworth's smashing blow. The instant he was clear, Wentworth squatted, snatched up the knife. If his reasoning was correct—and he had gambled his life on that fact—this man would not dare to kill him. His orders would be to bring Wentworth in alive and the leader's orders were usually obeyed to the letter. Had not that killer who had come for Caroline Davis feared his chief more than he feared the much-dreaded Spider?

Knife grasped in his hand, then, Wentworth crouched and

waited, ears strained for the first sound of attack. He could hear the whistling breath of the man he had struck, but since his blow had not been strong enough, this false Spider could move soundlessly to overwhelm him again. It would be child's play to strike down Wentworth from behind and carry him away. A blind man would be simple prey.

Swift as the thought, Wentworth's knife-hand swept upward. The palmed blade sang through the air. He heard a choked cry as the man dodged, then a grunt of pain. Wentworth snatched the bandage from his eyes and charged in the wake of his throw. He could make out the shadowy crouched figure of his assailant, a blur against the bright light of windows. Then he was upon the man, striking with both hands.

The killer lashed back at him, but only with one hand. It was clear that he had given up the battle, that he was more intent on escape than capture. Up to this moment, the fight had been almost soundless but now in their struggles the two smacked a chair to the floor. It caromed into a table and sent crockery crashing against the wall.

Wentworth was fighting blindly. That first glimpse against the light had turned into stabbing pain that blotted out all vision. Half his punches failed to land. A blow between the eyes sent him reeling backward. He heard glass shiver, heard a man's feet thud to the earth outside, then pound off into quick silence. He stood, brace-legged, his hands covering the fiery torment of his eyes, remained that way until he heard the door yanked open, heard the doctor's sharp voice.

Thereafter a man-nurse stayed in the room with Wentworth;

for two days he remained helpless. His demands for Kirkpatrick brought only word that his friend was busy working on the case and would return at the first opportunity. Twice Wentworth tried to slip out of the doctor's house but his blindness defeated him, forced him to remain inactive, fuming at the delay.

HE HAD not dared have police follow the trail of blood that he knew must lead from the window. He was positive that the knife he had thrown had pierced either the false Spider's left arm or his shoulder because the man had thrown only right-handed blows at him in the struggle.

Finally Kirkpatrick came to the doctor's house and the sound of his feet was weary as he entered. Wentworth heard a chair squeak as he dropped heavily into it. For a long moment silence held between the two, silence that Kirkpatrick was the first to break.

"Sorry I took so long, Dick," he said slowly, "but much has happened. Nita's price cards told me to call a certain phone number at a certain hour. She had noticed the auto fatalities and wanted to call them to your attention. She was crazy to come to see you, but I persuaded her it would be dangerous because of police surveillance." He drew a deep breath. "Apparently, the killer's men succeeded in following us the other day, or saw me and guessed that I would bring you to my doctor. I'm talking now about the visit of the Spider."

Wentworth frowned behind the bandage that covered his eyes. He had a feeling that Kirkpatrick was holding back something, that he talked of these trivial details while his mind was upon something else.

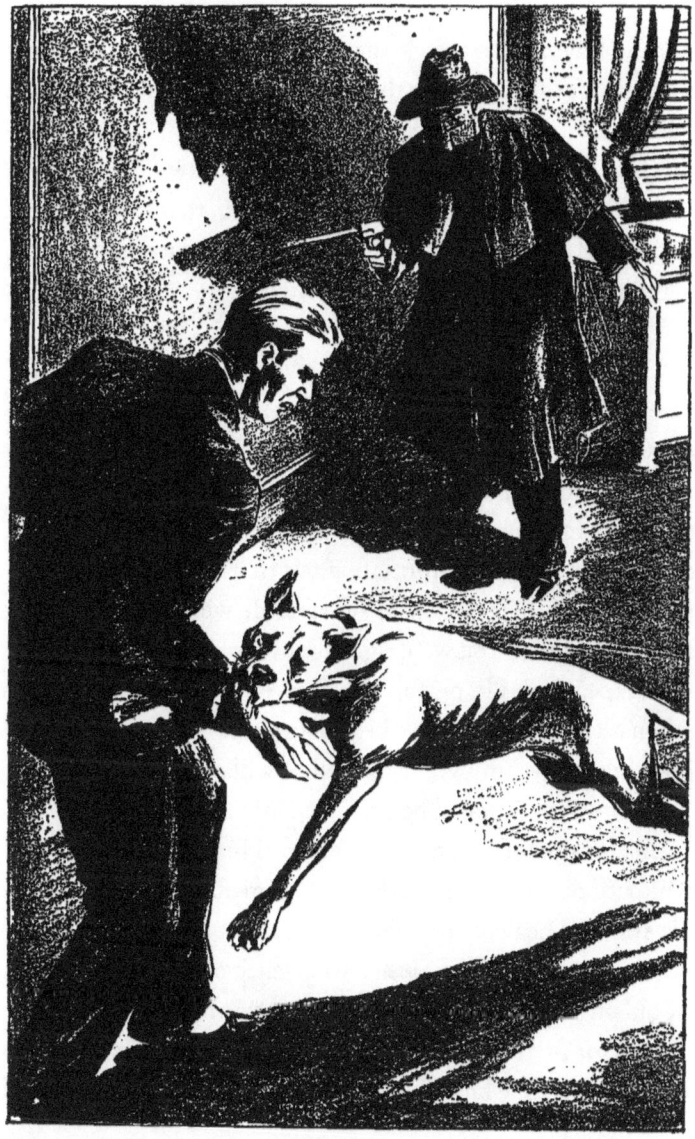

Wentworth whirled; his gun blasted. Apollo snarled and Hayes screamed.

"The killers have struck again," Wentworth said, guessing shrewdly at the reason for the restraint. "What have they done this time?"

Kirkpatrick was silent a long moment and when finally he spoke his words were slow. "I wanted to keep that from you," he said, "but I see there's no use. An excursion boat was sunk last night and seventy-five people drowned."

Wentworth started to his feet with a cry of rage.

"And you tell me to sit here and twiddle my thumbs all day!" he exclaimed. "I must get out of here. There are things to be done!"

"That isn't all," said Kirkpatrick wearily. "Two officials of the Atlas Insurance Company have committed suicide apparently. Boise gave the information out that way. They left statements giving their proxies to Bowfee. He will win control. But I suspect murder. You were right about his having a hand in the skyscraper deal. He put up about seventy-five percent of the purchase money. But I have been able to trace none of the criminal violence to him. We're up against a blank wall."

Wentworth dropped heavily back into his chair.

The tension of his anger still gripped him, but he knew that Kirkpatrick was determined to keep him out of the battle until his eyes had healed. They were much improved, but the doctor said using them might cause a recurrence of his blindness that would prove permanent. Two more weeks of being blindfolded, the doctor prescribed. Wentworth twisted in his chair. In two weeks, God alone knew how many more lives might be snuffed out by these vicious killers. He must pretend to be content to wait, cause these guards to relax their watch.

"If only I had my sight," cried Wentworth, "but without it I am utterly helpless."

"Yes, you are, Dick," Kirkpatrick said eagerly.

"You must keep out of the fight until you can see again. You must realize that."

Wentworth nodded his head as if in resignation.

"Heaven help these killers when I do get my sight back again!" he said.

He heard Kirkpatrick rise. "The doctor is doing everything he can to fix them up fast, Dick," he said. "But he says premature exposure to light may blind you forever. I'll keep in touch as often as I can. I'm calling Nita again tonight at the number her price tags indicate. Is there any message you want to send her?"

"Tell her there's no use in hiding any longer," he said. "She's to go back home. Apparently, the killers are no longer interested in removing Caroline Davis. Her story now supports the accusers of the Spider."

"You're sure of that, Dick?" Kirkpatrick asked.

WENTWORTH LAUGHED bitterly. "Do you think that if they wanted to find Caroline Davis they would fail to do so?" he snarled. "Even the police had little trouble in finding Nita."

"I guess you're right," Kirkpatrick agreed slowly.

"Your lawyer has been trying to get Jackson and Jenkyns and Ram Singh out of prison, but so far Boise and his associates have succeeded in blocking every move."

Wentworth nodded. "Okay. Don't forget to tell Nita what

I said. And tell her not to worry about me. I'll see her before very long."

Kirkpatrick left and Wentworth sat without moving for nearly an hour. Then he called to the man who watched over him, asked for water. As he waited, his hand strayed over a small table at his side, found a heavy book end. When the man held out the water, Wentworth swung the book-end... Two minutes later a silent shadow of a man slipped from a window and groped his way across the grounds that surrounded the doctor's house. A drug store called a taxicab for him. The driver's eyes guided him to Nita van Sloan's apartment.

Nita's Great Dane, Apollo, greeted his entrance with a soft joyful bark, bounded up to place his mighty paws upon his master's shoulders. Wentworth thumped him on the chest. There was joy in his greeting, too, for he had trained the huge dog from puppyhood. The intelligent animal would do his bidding. Once more, the Spider would have eyes he could trust.

Swiftly Wentworth moved about the familiar apartment with the dog ever at his heels. He found a kit of his tools in a secret compartment in the wall baseboard. He found holsters and guns to fit them and he found the long black cape, the mask and the broad-brimmed hat of the Spider. He made these into a bundle, tapped out a note for Nita on her typewriter, and left with his hand on Apollo's collar.

With Apollo to guide him, he walked four blocks from Nita's apartment and climbed into a taxicab. "Jack Hayes' gymnasium," he told the driver, giving the address. Then he leaned back, hand on the massive head of the dog, and smiled. If it came to an emergency, he might use his eyes briefly, but aside from that, he could not see. Alone and blind, the Spider was faring forth to battle the enemies of humanity!

Twice Wentworth had been upon the point of confiding his suspicions, of Gentleman Jack Hayes to Kirkpatrick, but each time be had refrained. An open investigation of the athletics *salon* would do no good. Hayes would acknowledge that untoward things had occurred, that Sidney Cartwright had been killed there. Then he would point out that it was impossible to control all the persons who came to his establishment. The old runaround—Kirkpatrick's investigation would have got nowhere. This was the type of job that only the Spider could do. It must be done at once.

Kirkpatrick had said that it was impossible to trace works of violence to Bowfee although they assisted his deals. That meant only one thing: another member of the gang directed that phase of operations. Jack Hayes' situation would be perfect for such work. Many men came and went for his gymnasiums every day, thus providing contacts. He was compelled to use all types of men as trainers, rubbers, attendants for various duties. These would provide the nucleus for his gang. Yes, Hayes was due to answer a few questions for the Spider.

WENTWORTH ALIGHTED a block from the gymnasium, walked to a rear entrance. He paused there long enough to toss his cape across his shoulders, to draw the mask over his face, to pull the broad-brimmed hat down upon his brows. Then, with Apollo pressing, against his thigh, he stole into the building. He knew where Hayes' offices were located and made his way there, pressed his ear against the outer door to listen. Within, all was silence. The knob turned without a sound beneath his hand. He let Apollo take the lead then and crossed to an inner door of ground glass that bore no sign. That room, too, was silent. Wentworth entered and sat behind a broad desk. He held down one of Hayes' pen-holders for Apollo to sniff, then settled himself to wait—with a gun in his hand.

It was an hour later that Apollo stiffened beneath his touch, and pulling away, moved soundlessly across the office. The door clicked open, shut again and Apollo growled softly. So, then, Jack Hayes had entered. The dog's sense of smell identified him. Wentworth's hand tightened on his automatic, invisible beneath the edge of the desk, as he pictured the sleek, tall elegance of Gentleman Jack poised glowering in the doorway.

"What's the big idea," Hayes asked softly from the doorway, "of coming here in that rig-out? Just because I let you wear it once doesn't make you the Spider. Answer me, fool!"

Wentworth let his lips part in a tight smile.

With his first words, Hayes had admitted his guilt, had admitted that he directed the activities of the false Spider. For it was obvious that he had mistaken Wentworth for the man who, at least once, had imitated him for the criminal ring. Wentworth lifted the barrel of his gun above the edge of the desk.

"Don't move, Hayes," he hissed softly. "You have made a slight mistake. I am not your miserable hireling. I am the real Spider!"

He heard Hayes' breath suck in.

"Watch him, Apollo." Wentworth told the dog, then laid his automatic on the desk. He leaned back in the chair. The Great

Dane would be better able to watch than he. The dog could see, and had been trained to attack if a man he was ordered to watch made a hostile move.

"There is some mistake," Hayes murmured hesitantly. "I have done nothing to deserve the attentions of the Spider."

Apollo snarled nastily and Hayes cursed under his breath. Wentworth laughed.

"I would advise you, Hayes, to try no tricks," he said. "Apollo has been well trained."

"But damn it, man," Hayes was vehement. "I tell you there is some mistake."

Wentworth leaned forward, tapped a lean forefinger on the desk. "Yes," he agreed softly, "but the mistake was yours. You spoke too quickly when you entered. Hayes, I know everything. I know why you are burning tenements all over town—all insured by Atlas. I know why excursion boats are being sunk, why Robert Kenton and his daughter were murdered.

"Incidentally, Hayes… How would you like to die the same way Kenton died?"

Hayes was utterly silent. Wentworth had no way of telling how his words had affected the man, how his threat of torture would make the man react. He only knew that at least Hayes had made no threatening move because Apollo was silent. Good Lord! If only he could *see*… but it would take more than this to make him risk permanent blindness by uncovering his eyes.

"Because, Hayes," Wentworth continued, "unless you give me a few items of information, I shall be forced to inflict on you, the same tortures that were used on Kenton."

HAYES SAID hoarsely. "In God's name, no…! But his voice did not sound frightened. It seemed—mocking. What treachery could the man be planning before the Spider's sightless eyes? Wentworth tensed forward, gun in his hand, ears straining for a hint of what threatened. He heard an infinitesimal sound, the rasp of a doorknob. It came from his left flank.

Wentworth whirled and his gun blasted in his hand. Apollo snarled and Hayes screamed. Where the door knob had squeaked, glass crashed to the floor and a man coughed tearingly with a bullet in his lung. Deliberately Wentworth sent a second bullet winging after the first.

He sprang then toward the spot whence Hayes' screams continued to rend the air. He groped and found Apollo's collar, felt that the Dane's teeth were sunk in the wrist of the man he had been told to watch. Wentworth's lips parted in a tight smile.

"You should know better than to go for a gun, Hayes," he said. "When a trained dog is watching you."

He caught Hayes by the collar, told Apollo sharply to let go and yanked the man to his feet.

"You and I are going out of here, Hayes," he said, then his voice rasped. "And if any of your men see us, God help you."

Wentworth thrust his prisoner through the door, stopped for a moment there though the clamor of shouting men was ringing through the halls, paused and printed on the ground glass the crimson seal of the Spider. The killers should know who had struck into their midst, who had snatched one of the leaders from his stronghold.

He halted only an instant, then he thrust Hayes ahead again.

"Remember," he ground out. "If one of your men so much as glimpses us, I'll—" he shook the man sharply by the collar, "turn the dog loose on you."

Hayes said, "For God's sake, no…" and this time there was no mockery in his voice. "I can't keep them from seeing us."

Wentworth laughed and his voice was hard and fierce. "Yet, the other night when I was trapped here, your men got out without wading through the mob. No, Hayes, it won't work. Either you take me out of here, secretly, or—*the dog!*"

He felt Hayes cringe and he stirred Apollo to a snarl with his foot.

"I think," Wentworth drawled, "that Apollo would enjoy having you at his disposal."

"Quickly, this way," Hayes gabbled. He tugged against Wentworth's restraining hand, turned left. Together they strode rapidly along echoing corridors while the shouting of Hayes' men grew dimmer behind them. Wentworth caught the stench of the locker rooms, the wet warmth of the showers as they passed, then Hayes paused.

"I've got to get keys out of my pocket," he quivered. "Don't let your dog bite me again."

"Get your keys," Wentworth said, gripping Apollo's collar with his gun-hand. In answer, the dog threw all his weight against the leather band. A vicious snarl rolled in his throat. He pulled loose from Wentworth and the crash of a pistol shot rang deafeningly. Wentworth reeled back a pace, his face stiff and hot from powder burn, but he had not been struck.

Apollo was snarling with a note of frustration.

Wentworth moved swiftly toward him. His hand found his collar, gropingly discovered that the dog was rearing against a door. The shouting was louder now. Men were pounding along the twisting corridors of the building toward him. Wentworth seized the knob of the door and lead slammed through the wood, plucked at his long cape. He was trapped. Hayes on one side of the door with his gun. On this side, men raced to kill him. **WENTWORTH YANKED** out his gun and poured lead through the closed door. "Run, boy," he gasped to Apollo. "Run!" He had kept careful track of his movements through the building. As nearly as he could figure it, he was on the second floor on the north side. The steps were fifty feet ahead and to the right. But could he reach them before he was spotted by his pursuers?

A shot answered him. He could not. Lead winged past him with an angry buzz. But the bullet sped from behind. At least he had a clear path ahead.

Po-oww! That gun had spoken from dead ahead!

Killers behind him, killers ahead.

Wentworth dragged Apollo to a halt and the rage that snarled in the dog's throat found an echo in his own. If he had his sight, his guns could answer. He whipped to the right, close against the wall, groping for an opening that should be near. A bullet thumped into the plaster wall by his hand and white dust stung his face. Apollo was straining against his hold, eager for the battle.

Abruptly, Wentworth's groping hand pushed through an opening. He flung into the cover, heard another bullet screech past. He doubled back to his right, found stairs that led upward and sought again Hayes' office. Judgment told him that there he would find the key to the escape passage. He should never have permitted Hayes to leave that spot, for it was certain that the man would have so arranged the hidden exit that he himself was always sure of safe retreat.

Wentworth flung into the office, stopped motionless, listening. He heard wheezing breath. The man he had shot! In three strides, Wentworth was beside him.

"The cops are here!" he cried. "Hayes has run away and left us! Where's the escape passage?"

The wheezing breath faltered.

"Here, I'll carry you," Wentworth said hurriedly. He caught the man beneath the arms, heaved him up. "For God's sake, be quick!" he said urgently. "The cops have already broken in."

"It's—no—use," the man gasped. "I'm—done for. So are you. Passage through safe. Can't open."

Through the safe! Wentworth eased the dying man to the floor, sprang into a groping circuit of the walls of the room. He found a window, a filing cabinet, three chairs, and three doors, but no safe. He cursed under his breath as he returned to the spot where the wounded man lay, then he stiffened, listening. He heard Hayes' shouting orders: "Upstairs, I tell you," Hayes howled. "He's bound to be upstairs. Every door was plugged. Up and get him. It's the real Spider!"

Wentworth smiled thinly and his nimble fingers reloaded his automatic. He dropped a hand and Apollo thrust his cold muzzle into it. Kirkpatrick was right, he thought regretfully. A blind Spider could not cope with these killers.

He heard the pounding of feet in the hall, crouched with gun ready, blind eyes turned toward the door....

CHAPTER 9
MASS MURDERS

E VEN AS Wentworth prepared to sell his life as dearly as possible in a last battle with the killers, ready to risk blindness now that he was trapped, an idea gnawed at the back of his brain. In his circuit of the room, his hands had found an unusual thing, something he had not noticed on his previous friendly visits to this office.

There was no longer a racing of feet in the hallways and he knew the killers were closing in upon these offices silently. They would rush the two doors at once, try to burn him down before his vicious guns could speed them to sudden death. Through two doors... abruptly Wentworth whirled toward the third wall of the room. He knew now what that unusual thing was which his sensitive hands had discovered. It was the third door of the room—three doors when he remembered only two.

He sprang toward the spot where he had found that third door and his exploring hands found a sliding panel of steel. The safe! It had been only a dummy after all, a false door to hide the secret exit. He felt the pressure of the dog's great body against his thigh and his hand flew over the surface of the door. Within seconds, he was through the opening, the door closed behind him, and with Apollo to lead, he hurried down steep stairs.

Two minutes later he was out on the street, following the

dog swiftly away from Hayes' stronghold. He had learned, at least, that his suspicions were correct that Hayes was connected with the killers, but bitter fury burned within him. The Spider had been forced to flee for his life where usually he would have wreaked vengeance and smashed the organization. Yet he knew that, even had he had his sight, it would have been well, this time, to seek safety in flight.

Hayes was one of the killers but he was not the master of the assassins. It would have been futile to risk death at the hands of underlings when the brain that directed them was still undiscovered—still free to work mischief. Let him once find the master criminal, and Wentworth would return, blind or not, to try conclusions with Hayes and his murderous crew.

Within the next hour, Wentworth changed taxis three times, but each time he bored farther northward through city traffic. It was midnight when he drew to a halt at last before a small unpretentious hotel in Yonkers.

"I have a reservation here," he told the clerk "The name is Caspar Clark."

"Ah, yes, indeed, Mr. Clark. Your wife and sister are here already. Front! Room three sixty-five. Yes, indeed, Mr. Clark."

Two minutes later, the door of his room closed behind him—and Nita van Sloan's arms were about his shoulders.

"Dick, oh, Dick," she whispered. "Your poor eyes!"

Wentworth laughed as joy and strength flowed into him. "Damn my eyes!" he said softly. "If only my blindness did not keep me from seeing your dear face. I think, though, that I still can find your lips!"

135

Nita laughed, too, and he knew from the sound that she was flushed with the embarrassment of love. "Dick!" she protested. "You forget your sister is here."

Wentworth turned, swept a bow. "Ah, yes, my sister!"

It was Caroline Davis' voice that broke the short abashed silence that followed; Caroline Davis who for the present was posing as "Caspar Clark's" sister just as Nita was posing as his wife—following the instructions Wentworth had left at Nita's apartment.

"I think," Wentworth said gravely to Caroline, "that I can promise you an end to your troubles. Within the hour, I shall get in touch with Arthur Merriwell."

The girl objected. "But you must not think of my little problems when so much greater difficulties are ahead of you."

Wentworth shook his head, smiling. "They are one," he told her. "When all your problems are solved, mine will be, too. Just now, I need Arthur's help."

IT WAS with Arthur's help that, an hour later, they all were seated in the library of Phineas Merriwell's mansion, but Wentworth soon discovered that he would have been equally welcome if he had come alone. He had risked everything to come in his own identity, and found the action wise. The aged millionaire abruptly dismissed the others save Arthur, who stayed at his own and Wentworth's request.

Since Cartwright's death, Merriwell said, he had investigated his affairs and found that, even as Wentworth and Arthur had suspected, the lawyer had embezzled hundreds of thousands of dollars from him. He had resumed active control of his business then, and immediately was embroiled in a dozen fights. He had ransomed the Atlas Insurance Company from Bowfee's schemes, had thrown his millions to the support of the automobile company which had been driven nearly to bankruptcy by the planting of defective material among its supplies. In fact, he had done already all that Wentworth had come to request of him—that he use his resources to battle the Murder Trust financially, while Wentworth fought to halt their criminal enterprises.

"It seems to me," Wentworth told him in the end, "that the sinking of your excursion ship may be a direct attack upon you in answer to your maneuvers."

Phineas Merriwell grunted and there was an edge to his kindly old voice as he replied.

"I would agree with you but for one thing—tonight three other excursion boats sank. I think the total loss of life is something like five hundred souls!"

Wentworth sat in stunned silence for a moment while the fearful purport of that information sank home. Even then, the only sign he gave was the tense closing and opening of his hands. He sat bolt upright, his face stiff with horror.

Five hundred human lives had been snuffed out to satisfy the selfish lust of the Murder Trust. Here, again, the motive was obscure. Men, women, and children had been plunged to a watery death so that the monster who directed the killers might line his pockets with gold.

Wentworth jumped to his feet. "By God, Mr. Merriwell!" he cried. "These last five hundred murders have signed their death warrants!"

For a full minute after Wentworth's bitter cry rang through the room, utter silence reigned. Then Phineas Merriwell's thin old voice asked an incisive question.

"How?"

Wentworth sat slowly down again. He felt the strained attentions of the millionaire and his son. "We'll let them sink one more boat—or rather try to. We'll invite a number of prominent people on a trip on one of your excursion boats to investigate these disasters. You and I will go along—*as bait!*"

Merriwell said slowly. "I don't believe I understand."

WENTWORTH LEANED forward, tapping a lean forefinger into the palm of his hand. "You and I," he said, "are the two persons above all others in the world whom these men would like to sweep from their path. You, because of your financial warfare with their leaders. I, because they think I am the Spider, the one man they fear. We will offer ourselves as bait by taking an advertised trip on a boat such as they have already destroyed. When they strike, we will have a surprise ready for them, a surprise that will end in their capture and death."

Wentworth straightened and smiled. "I'll do another little piece of advertising, at the same time I spread rumors about going on the trip," he said. "I'm going to let it be known that I have the evidence to convict the man who has been posing as the Spider at all these horrible crimes. That evidence will be valid only so long as I am alive. When I die, that evidence will die with me."

Merriwell said slowly. "That seems a very dangerous kind of evidence to hold."

Wentworth's mouth tightened. "It is."

"And you actually have evidence to prove that the real Spider did not commit these crimes?" Arthur Merriwell asked, breathlessly.

Wentworth nodded. "Yes, but I can't use that evidence until I have caught the false Spider himself, and wiped out the gang with which he works." He hesitated. "It seems callous to suggest that you offer yourself as bait, but I honestly can see no other way of snaring these men. There is no way of telling when or where they will strike next. Only if we set the target ourselves can we be ready to trap them."

Merriwell sat silent for a long time, his youthfully blue eyes peering through his antique glasses at Wentworth. From time to time, he nodded. Finally he stretched out a thin, blue-veined hand and clasped Wentworth's arm firmly, "I'm in it, Wentworth," he said, with a note of exultation in his voice. He laughed, then, and his wrinkled face seemed more alive. "By God, it's been a long time since I've fought. But they'll find out there's sap in the old trunk yet."

During the ensuing days of preparation, Wentworth remained in hiding under the doctors' care. He made only two suggestions for the list of guests. Emile Bowfee and Howard Boise, the Commissioner of Police. Bowfee agreed immediately, but Boise refused until the newspapers printed the Spider's promise to attend.

Boise's acceptance was a quiet pledge that if the Spider was on the boat, he would be captured—or killed!

It was singular that once the trip was announced, not a single crime occurred which could be traced to the Murder Trust. It was as if, given an opportunity of wiping out the opposition at one fell swoop, the killers preferred to wait for that occasion—and meantime to do nothing to frighten their prey from the trap. As the day neared, Wentworth felt an increasing, almost physical tension.

His own preparations were simple. He and Merriwell planned to have an arsenal aboard the boat. They were to have a picked crew, and at the crucial moment when the killers attacked, these men would be armed to wipe out the cohorts of the Murder Trust.

"I am gambling, of course, that the leaders will direct the attack in person," Wentworth told Merriwell when, the night before the trip, they conferred briefly. "But I am pretty sure that they will come. They've made a number of attacks on me and all of them have failed so far because their subordinates slipped up. This time, though, the big leaders will probably come along to make sure that you and I die."

WENTWORTH SMILED wryly; Merriwell nodded his snowy crown of hair in serious agreement. Through the darkened glasses that he wore, Wentworth could see him clearly. The few days of waiting had not been wasted, for the doctor had practically finished curing his eyes. However, Wentworth was concealing that fact, even in Merriwell's home, where he had come under the triple guard that Kirkpatrick insisted on providing. There was always the chance that the spies of the Murder Trust had penetrated here.

"Yes," Merriwell broke into the silence that followed Wentworth's statement, "they will most certainly try to make sure that we die."

Wentworth frowned. "There's no denying the risk," he said slowly. "And the risk is greater for you than it is for me. I'm used to risking my life. It is my job. Yours is to remain alive and fight with your money. And—pardon me for saying it—if the boat were sunk, it would be much easier for me to escape than for you with your infirmities."

Wentworth leaned forward. "I really don't believe it's necessary for you to go," he said. "So long as publicity states that you are going, the killers will attack us. It is not as though you were active physically and could participate in the battle."

Merriwell smiled slightly. "What you are saying is that I would be in the way with my wheel chair and my useless legs." He brushed aside Wentworth's quick protest. "You are right about that, of course," he acknowledged, "but who would take charge of the affair? Frankly, I'd rather go."

"Your duty is not to go," Wentworth snapped.

"As for taking charge, why not invite Emile Bowfee to take command?"

There was argument, but in the end, about midnight, Wentworth called Bowfee and, identifying himself as Merriwell's secretary, urged that Bowfee take command. The publisher refused flatly.

"Not that I don't appreciate the honor," he said, "but the entire affair is Merriwell's plan and he should direct it. I'm sorry he's not feeling well"—that was the excuse Wentworth had given—"but I think it would be better to postpone the trip rather than that Merriwell should not go along. I'll drop by in the morning, and if he isn't well enough to go, we'll just call the thing off."

When Wentworth conveyed that message to Merriwell, the aged millionaire's eyes gleamed.

"That's very kind of him," he murmured. "But if I were of a suspicious nature, I would say he was in cahoots with the killers and wanted to make sure I would be there to die!"

Wentworth nodded slowly. "There is reason enough to suspect Bowfee," he agreed, "but there's nothing to connect him with any of the violence. We can't act against him until we are sure."

Merriwell leaned his anemic body tensely forward in his armed chair. "Perhaps, after tomorrow," he said. "We will be sure! We'll keep a careful watch on Bowfee throughout the trip."

Wentworth agreed. "We must be ready for treachery among our guests by all means."

He rose to go and the big double doors of the room opened with such abruptness that he started, whirled around alertly, half expecting attack. It was Arthur Merriwell and Caroline Davis. The girl was running.

"Father Merriwell!" she cried. "I don't want you to go on that trip tomorrow. I have a premonition about it—"

"It's nonsense, dear," Arthur broke in, his serious young face worried. "It's just an ordinary trip of inspection, and there couldn't possibly be any danger."

"But all these boats blowing up and sinking recently!" The girl turned from Wentworth and Merriwell to argue with the boy, who above her fiery hair, looked at his father and smiled slightly. "Besides," said the girl. "If there isn't any danger, I want to go."

"What she's really up to," Arthur said quietly, "is that she wants to be there to help the Spider if he needs it. She's read his promises to attend and knows about Boise's threat."

MERRIWELL CHUCKLED. "Well, why not let her go along then?" he asked, but he winked as he said it. So it was arranged, with the covert understanding, that that girl would be diverted somehow at the last minute. Wentworth made his adieux, groping blindly for the door and finally going out on Arthur's arm.

Caroline took his other arm and as they approached the door, she stumbled, lurched against Wentworth, and as he caught her, he heard the hurried sibilance of whispering.

"Nita phoned that your guards are Torture Killers," Caroline breathed. "She said to tell you secretly."

Wentworth steadied the girl and his face remained utterly impassive, though his pulses raced to the call of danger. He knew what Caroline meant as if she had told him in great detail. In some way, Nita had got wind of a plot to assassinate him by substituting killers for the guards that Kirkpatrick had insisted on giving him. Caroline and Arthur had staged their little show merely that he might be informed of it secretly. The fact that the killers knew of his trip to the house was proof enough that there were spies among Merriwell's many servants.

"You weren't hurt, my dear?" was his only response to Caroline's news.

"No." The girl was a little breathless. "And you?" Wentworth

143

smiled quietly. "It will take more than that to harm me, Caroline," he said. "I'll thank you very much if you'll see me to my car now."

"But—" the girl began.

Wentworth squeezed her arm. "It's quite all right," he said. "I'll see you in the morning."

He entered the car calmly, settled back on the cushions as a man climbed in beside him, There were two others in the front seat, but none had taken the trouble to disguise himself. What was the use when their victim was blind?

"Home," Wentworth ordered quietly. The car purred forward.

Out of the corner of his eye, Wentworth looked at the man beside him. His face was visible in the diminishing lights from the house. He was grinning evilly. He held an automatic leveled at Wentworth's side.

CHAPTER 10
BEWARE THE LAMB!

WENTWORTH'S FACE was utterly expressionless although he read death in the leer of the man beside him. Only one question remained in his mind. Did the fellow intend to kill him out of hand, or would he be taken to some selected spot and executed before the leaders? The leveled gun seemed to settle that. His death was the only thing the leaders cared about.

A glance at the two men ahead showed that one had twisted around to stare toward him. His right hand rested on the back of the seat and held a gun also. Yes, these two had been scheduled to kill him at once. But how had Nita got wind of the situation? Wentworth shook his head. No way of telling, but he felt somehow that the information was of vast importance.

"Light me a cigarette, please," Wentworth said casually to the man beside him. He could tell by the man's hesitation that the simple request had disconcerted him.

"Come, come," Wentworth said sharply. "A cigarette. Are you deaf? You know I can't see to light one for myself."

He heard the crinkle of cellophane as the man fumbled with a package, then the sputter of the match. Its dim moment of light showed the gun resting on the seat beside the man. Wentworth's hand moved with lightning rapidity. He caught up the weapon and fired as his fingers closed about the butt. The gangster in the forward seat, lurched forward as the bullet took him in the side of the head. The chauffeur cursed. Brakes squealed and his hand flashed to his gun.

Wentworth's lips were smiling grimly. He jerked the captured automatic aside as the man beside him recovered from his surprise and grabbed for it. The pistol swung horizontally in a swift arc, crunched against the gangster's forehead. The chauffeur had his weapon now, but it did him small good. Even as he whirled, slowing the car to a stop, Wentworth fired again.

The driver slammed forward upon the steering wheel, collapsed limply. Wentworth was out of the car in a second, hauling out the two dead men. It was the work of moments to spill the corpses into the ditch and print his warning crimson seal upon their foreheads. Then he jerked the unconscious man to the front seat, took the wheel and raced ahead. It was possible that convoying cars had been sent to make sure of his death.

Three miles further on, he decided that if such had been the case, his swift attack had forestalled the reinforcements. He whirled from the road into a woodsy side-lane where the car was soon masked from view by thick shrubbery. He hauled his prisoner out on the ground then and slapped him back to consciousness.

The man attempted to jerk to his feet as his senses came back to him, but Wentworth thrust him down in the white path of the headlights and the assassin lay flat upon his back and quivered. His lips trembled with fright and he stared with terrified eyes into the mouth of the automatic Wentworth leveled at his forehead.

"I have a trade to propose to you," said Wentworth quietly. "Some information for your life."

"What do you want to know?" the man gabbled.

Wentworth could scarcely credit the killer's prompt surrender, but he threw swift questions at him.

"What are your leader's plans for tomorrow?" he demanded.

"Dey're going to blow up de boat," the man gasped, his eyes fixed on the muzzle of the ready automatic.

"Why did they try to kill me tonight then?"

"De boss is afraid you'd queer de game tomorrow," the man said readily. "But there ain't no need to ask me who de boss is 'cause I don't know. I gets my orders from Tiff what you blew a hole in just before you conked me."

WENTWORTH STARED down at the prostrate man

speculatively. He seemed too frightened to lie. The death of his two companions had completely unnerved him.

"There is more to it than that," Wentworth said quietly. "Some additional reason why they don't want me on the boat." The man lay unmoving; tremors of fear still shook him. Still Wentworth was not satisfied with the explanation. It was possible that Bowfee was the leader and had wanted to make sure that Wentworth would get no chance to kill him when the attack on the steamer began.

Once more Wentworth considered the possibility of a man-to-man showdown with Bowfee for evidence certainly pointed strongly to him as the leader of the Murder Trust. Once more he discarded the idea. Guilty the publisher might be, but he undoubtedly had partners in crime. There was no way to root them all out except to compel the entire force to take the field and to meet them in open battle. Tomorrow's kills should be important enough to the Murder Trust to bring them all out, including the leaders. Tonight's fiasco would make them the more determined to wipe out the Spider, would make them realize anew the futility of sending lesser minions against him.

"Listen, boss," the gangster whined. "I want to make a deal. I know something. I… *Gees!* Boss!" The muzzle of the automatic was grinding against his forehead. "I said I'd talk!"

"You certainly will," the Spider rasped. "Spill it!"

"Tiff said he was to help bump the Mayor soon as he got the flash from the boat!" The man spluttered his words with eager haste. "The Mayor and three other big nuts. Tiff says his boss

147

"I'm tired of your damned foolishness," Bowfee growled.

He lurched backward toward the water.

figures to take over the city. He owns four or five big guys and when these was bumped, he'd have clear sailing."

Wentworth felt the angry blood pulse through a thin knife-scar upon his temple, relic of a battle of long ago. Was there no limit to the infamous plans of these men? They planned to celebrate the extermination of their enemies on the steamer by seizing control of the city's coffers! They could milk the treasury of millions within a few short months.

He straightened slowly. "How do you mean, the flash from the boat?" he asked. "How will the signal be sent?"

The man pushed himself up to a sitting position. "I don't know, Boss," he said. "I told you just what Tiff told me, the guy you bumped."

Abruptly, the gangster flung himself at Wentworth's legs. They went down in a tangle together and the man wriggled free, sprang to the car and flung himself into the seat. Wentworth heard the starter grind, saw the car lurch toward him. He dived from its crushing path, snapped two shots through the windshield. The car swerved, rammed its nose against a tree and stalled.

Frowning heavily, Wentworth hauled the dead gangster from behind the wheel and drove away. There were many puzzling aspects of this attack.

Nita's fortuitous learning of the plans; the mans eager gush of information. Furthermore, he couldn't reconcile the plan to blow up the excursion boat with his suspicions of Bowfee and Boise. Was it possible that, after all, Bowfee and Boise were innocent?

Wentworth jerked his head sharply in the negative. He did

not believe his deductions could have gone awry. No, one of those two was responsible for this juggernaut of crime and death that had been flattening the public beneath its massive, bloody wheels.

WELL, AT least one of those questions could be answered immediately. He found a phone-booth and called Nita, learned that she had discovered the plot against his life when one of the guards, overpowered and left for dead, had recovered consciousness and phoned her. She could throw no more light on the situation. And Wentworth, making his way back to the home of the doctor where he had been hiding, pondered vainly over the situation.

It would be simple to post guards about the Mayor, but who were the other important officials that the Murder Trust planned to remove? There was no way of telling. Should the Spider trust to his arrangements on the boat to remove the killers, or should he guard the Mayor against harm? Slowly, a grim smile spread upon Wentworth's lips. The answer to that was obvious. If the Murder Trust and its cohorts failed to signal from the boat, the Mayor would be safe, the city and the pockets of its citizens would be safe from the thieving fingers of these killers. Then, the Spider would go upon the boat—and make sure that all the Murder Trust died!

The following morning, Wentworth became Professor Carter. He spent an hour over his disguise, and emerged from his rooms with the bowed shoulders of the student, the thin wild hair of the traditional absent-minded professor. His clothing was careless and shapeless and he interlarded his speech with Latin phrases.

Merriwell, when Wentworth arrived at his estate according to plan, greeted him marveling.

"Wonderful," he declared. "Absolutely wonderful! Come and let me introduce Bowfee. Our esteemed friend is anxiously waiting in the library, making sure that the lamb is led to the slaughter."

"Cave Agnum," said Wentworth gravely. "Beware the lamb!"

Merriwell laughed softly, but there was grimness just beneath the surface. He signed to the giant Negro behind his wheel chair and the three moved through broad double-doors into the library, Wentworth walking along with an absently shuffling gait.

"Professor Carter," Merriwell introduced him.

"An expert in dynamics who may prove useful in determining the cause of the wrecks."

Bowfee shook hands in silence while Wentworth babbled inconsequential things. The publisher's hand was small, strangely out of proportion to the man's six feet two. His deep voice rang heartily as he asked after Merriwell's health, and Wentworth studied him through dark glasses. The man had braced his bulky body, straddle-legged before the broad library windows. A black cigar was clamped between wide white teeth.

Bowfee ignored Wentworth after the initial remarks, talked gravely with Merriwell about the sunken excursion boats and the possibility that some human agency was behind the disasters. He did not think, said Bowfee, that any human being could be such a monster; furthermore, he did not believe in Master Minds. Now in his newspapers… His harangue lasted the entire distance to the wharf where the *City of Manhattan* was moored, where police held back crowds of staring people—and detectives searched for the Spider, whose pledge that he would make the trip had been published in all the newspapers.

The gigantic Negro picked up Merriwell like a baby and carried him aboard the steamer, past batteries of photographers. Wentworth passed the alertly watchful police without challenge and ten minutes later the boat whistled its way out into the river. WENTWORTH WANDERED with apparent aimlessness about the boat. Finally the clipped sharp voice of Kirkpatrick reached his ears, and he ambled toward his friend. Immediately he heard another voice he knew, that of Howard Boise, the present Commissioner of Police.

"I am curious," he heard Kirkpatrick say, and knew from the chill tone that there was no friendliness between the two. "I am curious to know why you carry your left arm in a sling, Boise."

Wentworth stopped, leaned on the railing, apparently staring out over the water. A sudden thought had tensed his body swelled the fighting muscles in his shoulders. Boise carried his left arm in a sling and—Wentworth had knifed the false Spider in the left arm! He listened acutely.

"I appreciate your solicitude," Boise sneered, "but I must insist that how I hurt my arm is none of your damned business."

"Be careful, Boise," Kirkpatrick said softly.

"Remember that Police Commissioners may be removed."

"Do you threaten me?" Boise's voice was still quiet. Wentworth recalled that the man never seemed hurried, never flustered by circumstance or mishap. Kirkpatrick's laughter was quiet, too, but there were overtones of meaning in his reply.

"I only state a fact, Boise," he said. "But I think it would be advisable for you to confide in me about your shoulder. It so happens that a very notorious criminal who always travels in disguise was stabbed in the left shoulder!"

Wentworth turned abruptly from the railing, deliberately blundered into the two men. He made profuse, absent-minded, apologies.

"My eyes are not of the best," he explained. "Oh, I hope I did not hurt your shoulder. Is it painful? How did you hurt it? Ah, it's bleeding. Come, let us find a doctor...."

He caught Boise by the arm and hustled him down the deck, leaving Kirkpatrick staring. He had caught familiar accents in the blurred, mild voice of that obvious professor, then that remark about poor vision... A slow smile spread across Kirkpatrick's lips.

Below decks, Wentworth found Boise obstinate. "I can do without your help!" he said stiffly. He jerked his arm clear of Wentworth's hand, strode into the doctor's quarters alone. Wentworth blundered after him, still apologizing. He was in time to hear Boise say:

"A stab wound and some blundering fool opened it again, doctor. Can you fix up a fresh dressing?"

His voice cut off. He snapped at Wentworth:

"Will you get the hell out of here? You've done enough damage already."

Wentworth babbled on, but drifted from the sick bay. He

sought Kirkpatrick, told him what he had learned. "A stab wound in the left shoulder doesn't mean he's the Spider," he concluded. "But at least it's suspicious. And there are other things that point toward Boise."

Kirkpatrick murmured an assent. "Apollo is in my cabin," he said. "I thought we might need his help before this day was over."

Wentworth put an affectionate hand on Kirkpatrick's arm. "What you mean, of course, is that my eyes may give out and I'll need Apollo to guide me." He gave his friend no chance to reply. "What do the crew look like?" he asked quickly. "Merriwell said they were all trustworthy men and good fighters."

Kirkpatrick grunted. "Good fighters, perhaps," he agreed, "but there isn't a man among them that I'd trust as far as a handcuff chain would let him go."

"The devil!" Wentworth smothered down a curse. "Let's go see Merriwell."

"Furthermore," Kirkpatrick said. "There isn't a life-boat or life-belt on board that would hold up a kitten. If this boat were to go down, only those who could swim would remain afloat—and I've a hunch they wouldn't last long."

"What do you mean, Kirk?" Wentworth asked tensely.

"I think Merriwell has been double-crossed, that the crew on here is not his, but—"

"Quick," Wentworth snapped. "Take me to Merriwell." He gripped Kirkpatrick's arm and they strode rapidly along to where the aged millionaire sat in a wheel-chair in the lee of a deck-house.

"The crew—" Wentworth asked harshly. "Are they your men?"

"They are not," Merriwell answered under his breath. "I've sent three men looking for you so I could tell you."

Wentworth grated out an oath. "There's no doubt of it," he swore. "Your crew are the *assassins of the Murder Trust!*"

A HEAVY footfall on the deck pulled Wentworth about tensely, then he forced the rigidity from his muscles and nodded vaguely to the big man who loomed beside him, Emile Bowfee.

"Anything the matter?" The voice of the publisher was hearty, but Wentworth thought he sensed mockery in it. He stuttered into a rambling account of bumping into Boise, how angry the Police Commissioner had been, how alarmed he was over the mishap.

"By the way," Kirkpatrick broke in on Wentworth's account, "you're a close acquaintance of Boise, aren't you, Bowfee? Tell us, how was he hurt? I'm sure he wasn't shot or we'd have heard of it in the papers."

The mocking quality of Bowfee's voice was still present when he replied. "It happened in Jack Hayes' gymnasium, I think. The button broke off a foil and the sharp end jabbed him in the shoulder. It was Hayes himself, as I recall, and they were fencing without plastrons."

Wentworth shuddered. "Bloodthirsty things, those foils," he murmured.

His mind was racing. If Boise actually was the false Spider, this would have been an excellent way to frame an excuse for his wound, to go to that ally of the Murder Trust, Jack Hayes, and fake an injury with a broken foil. That explanation was more suspicious than if none had been offered….

But there was no time to speculate on such a minor matter as that. Death at the hands of the assassins confronted them all, possibly within minutes. The substitute crew, the wrecked safety equipment proved that.

It seemed unlikely that the intention was simply a massacre of everyone aboard, otherwise there would have been no point in rendering all the boats and lifebelts useless. On the other hand, it was not probable that they planned to blow up the craft since their own men were aboard. No, something else was in the wind, but would could it be?

Wentworth jerked his head impatiently. It seemed impossible that these killers could outmaneuver him on every turn, yet with the single exception that he had contrived to escape their traps; that he had snatched from them the girl they planned to murder, they had beaten him continually. He pressed his palm heavily to his forehead. He must—must triumph today, or the Murder Trust would wipe out all opposition, and by killing the officials, have the city completely at its mercy.

Abruptly, Wentworth whirled, strode back to where he had left Bowfee and Merriwell. He slowed to a saunter, halted beside Kirkpatrick, who was staring out over the sun-sparkling waters.

"Kirk," Wentworth said without moving his lips. "I think it would be wise for you to take Apollo and guard the arsenal. If we keep that in control, our position will be stronger. I'll keep a close eye on Bowfee."

Kirkpatrick clipped out an assent and presently strolled away. Wentworth attached himself to Bowfee, began to ask questions about his newspapers. Though his nerves tingled with constant alertness for danger, though he knew that any moment might precipitate wholesale slaughter of the innocents whom he himself had brought aboard, Wentworth stayed calmly chatting with Bowfee on into the afternoon.

BOWFEE WAS palpably bored and tried to escape several times, but Wentworth hung on with the blind persistence of the character he had assumed. The boat was now nearing the scene of the major disaster of the series of excursion boat accidents. In a rising sea, the craft had run aground on rocky Beloe's reef and broken up before help could reach her.

The rocks were even now lifting black ugly teeth above the water a little over a mile ahead. There was no sea running today, but somehow, as the *City of Manhattan* drew nearer and nearer to those dread shoals that had taken a toll of one hundred and fourteen lives, Wentworth felt a slow tightening of the tension that had gripped him throughout the day. He noticed, too, that Bowfee seemed more irascible. He maintained a moody silence, ignoring Wentworth's questions and sucked noisily at an unlighted black cigar. He hunched himself up on the boat's port rail and sat upon it with his elbows resting on his knees. Wentworth eased up beside him diffidently.

"For Judas' sake!" Bowfee growled, "would you mind—"

"What is it?" Wentworth asked with the anxious amiability of the professor. "Is there something wrong?"

"I'm tired of your damned foolishness," Bowfee growled. "Move over!"

He shoved Wentworth violently and, at the same time, he lost balance and lurched backward toward the water. He let out a hoarse cry, arms waving wildly. Wentworth's left hand stabbed out and caught Bowfee's collar and he flung himself back. The man's weight was a terrific strain upon his hold and he seemed incapable of helping himself.

Abruptly, a huge form—Merriwell's Negro servant—stepped between Wentworth and the light. A moment later, Bowfee spilled to the deck. Wentworth staggered at the sudden release of weight, dropped on both knees and pitched forward on his hands. Masked by the fall, his right fist jabbed beneath Bowfee's chin and caught him on the larynx with a blow much used in *jiu-jitsu*. It paralyzed the man's throat and knocked him unconscious.

Wentworth scrambled to his feet. "Quick!" he gasped. "Mr. Bowfee has hurt his head. Carry him below." He turned toward Merriwell. "Let your man carry him."

The Negro lifted Bowfee easily and Wentworth following, directing the man to the arsenal. Bowfee was already beginning to stir when they entered the room, and at a word from Wentworth, Kirkpatrick and the Negro bound the publisher hand and foot. When his bull voice started to rip out again, Wentworth slid his fist against the already injured larynx, rocked the knuckles slowly back and forth. Bowfee's voice choked off.

"Don't shout," said Wentworth softly. "A whisper will be enough. Now, Bowfee, you are about to tell us your plans for killing us all."

"You're crazy," Bowfee snarled. "Listen, Kirkpatrick, take this crazy old coot away."

159

Kirkpatrick said dryly, "I'd advise you to talk. Crazy men have been known to torture people. And, as you can see, I'm helpless."

Bowfee roared out an oath and Wentworth's knuckles rocked his throat into silence again.

"Let's gag him, Kirk," he said wearily, "and leave him here."

"If the boat goes down," Kirkpatrick mused slowly, "he'll drown."

WENTWORTH LAUGHED softly. "Won't that be too bad?" he jeered. "Gag him, Kirk, then rig up a dummy and throw it overboard, a dummy of a man. Yell 'Man overboard!' and get excited about it."

Wentworth felt his way to a rack of weapons, took down two extra automatics which he shoved into his coat pockets to supplement those holstered beneath his arms.

"Why not just throw Bowfee overboard?" Kirkpatrick asked. "He'd die soon and it would save the trouble of making a dummy."

"Good God, man!" Bowfee exclaimed in hushed tones. "You can't do a thing like that! It would be murder!" Wentworth laughed sharply once. "No, Kirk, let's let him die by accident. Just leave him tied up here until the boat sinks! Bring Apollo in here to guard him. Apollo, not being tied, will be able to escape." He grinned. "Don't forget the dummy, Kirk, and yell 'Man overboard!' to beat all hell."

Wentworth turned toward the door, then hesitated. He was sure Bowfee had attempted to throw himself overboard. Why would he do that, save as a signal? Undoubtedly he wanted to leave the *City of Manhattan* before the killers' work began, and had planned to be picked up by some other boat. Yet Wentworth's threat to make the signal falsely, to leave Bowfee alone to drown seemed to make no impression on the man.

Was it possible, Wentworth asked himself once more, that he was wrong about Bowfee's guilt? The man's anxiety that Merriwell be on the steamer might have been legitimate, his reasons the ones he had given. Wentworth jerked his head in negative. Bowfee must be the man. The next half-hour would tell the story.

Wentworth, once outside the door, resumed the shambling loose-kneed gait of the professor, went on deck. Most of the passengers were grouped on the port deck and he could tell from their excited comments that the black rocks on which the previous ships had piled up were near at hand.

"A half-mile off yet," a man answered his question.

Suddenly a deep, excited voice rang along the decks. "Man overboard!" it shouted. "Man overboard!"

Kirkpatrick was doing his job well. It sounded convincing. Other voices caught up the cry, but the shout that Wentworth awaited did not come. From the bridge, an officer should call, "Where away?" From the bridge also should come orders to halt the boat, to turn back and pick up the man who had fallen overboard.

But none of these things happened.

Standing tensely, waiting, listening for some hint of the violence that impended, Wentworth became aware that the course of the ship was changing. But it was not turning to starboard, away from the coast to circle toward that supposed man in the water. It turned to port, toward the shore, toward....

With a hoarse cry, Wentworth fought his way through the streaming crowd of men who were rushing about the decks to stare back toward the spot where Kirkpatrick had tossed the dummy. It took minutes to get clear of the crowd, to reach a companionway leading upward. He took that in great strides, hauling himself toward the bridge with racing feet and gripping hands.

He knew now why Bowfee had tried to throw himself overboard. It was to distract the crowd while the boat turned the opposite way, while it rammed nose-on into that fatal reef of black rocks!

CHAPTER 11
ON BELOE'S REEF

THE RACE to the bridge of the boat seemed endless. Dashing passengers continually blocked him. And each second hurled them nearer to those grinning black fangs of rocks—and death.

A picture of the familiar spot flashed before Wentworth's eyes as he fought through a fresh panicky rush of people toward the last flight of steps that led upward to the bridge. Beloe's reef thrust up amid deep water, jagged black rocks with the constant white froth of foam about them like the ravening mouth of a beast. Behind them, a single larger ridge of rock reared like a table, but that was all.

The shore was three miles away. Boats and lifebelts were useless—and the crew were killers to a man. To make matters worse, dark clouds were obscuring the eastern sky and blotting out the daylight. If no one spotted the wrecked steamer during the next fifteen minutes, there would be no word that she had struck until morning. By that time, there would be only dead to greet the rescuers.

Wentworth sprang to the bridge, snatched at the door of the wheelhouse with his left hand, a gun in his right. Within, a revolver spat. The bullet crunched into the door by Wentworth's shoulder. He sped three bullets to answer that one. They were enough. No more shots spurted at him from the house.

Wentworth sprang to the wheel. "Afraid you came too late," the man panted, spinning the wheel. "That lubber stuck a gun in my ribs and made me hold on the reef."

"There's less than a hundred yards to go," Wentworth snapped. "You can't turn in time to keep from hitting. Hold your course and ram her on hard. That'll at least hold her nose up until help comes. Every life-boat on board has been scuttled."

"Scuttled!" A string of blistering oaths ripped from the man. Then he fell silent. He needed his breath for spinning the wheel. Wentworth sprang from the wheelhouse, sped downward. As he scrambled past the deck where the crowd still milled, a man screamed.

"The rocks!" he cried. "My God, the rocks."

Wentworth's face was grimly set. He was racing desperately for the arsenal. He whirled into a *salon*, down a companionway and along a narrow corridor between white-painted cabin doors. Feet pounded at the other end of the corridor, and Wentworth recognized Kirkpatrick, racing for the arsenal also.

"We're going to hit," Kirkpatrick yelled. Wentworth jerked a nod, reached the arsenal door and gripped the knob. He shouted at the dog on guard inside, lest the beast spring on him before recognizing his master.

"Down, Apollo," he cried.

As he twisted the knob, thrust the door in, Kirkpatrick skated to his side. Their gasp was one of shock and horror.

"Good God!" Kirkpatrick squeezed out the words. The great tan dog stood with lolling jaws that were stained with crimson. On the floor lay three men. Two of them were dead, their throats torn by the dog's fangs. The third was Bowfee, whom the two had tried to free. Bowfee was alive, but white with terror.

"Good dog, Apollo," Wentworth shouted. "Kirk, take Bowfee on deck and get him up on the table rock when we hit. I'll get more guns. Apollo, guard him!" He flung a hand at Kirkpatrick, then leaped to the gun racks. He knew what impended now. The slaughter of the innocents!

Those who were not drowned—and Wentworth believed that his move in sending the boat squarely and hard upon the rocks would prevent any deaths that way—were to be killed by the crew. Undoubtedly, all of those men had life belts hidden away. Undoubtedly, too, some other boats would be near, by pre-arrangement, to pick them up.

WENTWORTH STAGGERED from the arsenal, reached a companionway—and pitched forward heavily on his face. With a crunching crash, the boat went on the rocks. She shuddered and lifted at the nose. Timbers broke with an explosion-like cannon-fire. Waters roared into the smashed hold and

164

the hissing blast of steam came up from below. Above it all rose the shrieks and screams of frightened people. It was not alone that the boat was aground; it was the memory that on these rocks a hundred and fourteen mortals had perished miserably in just such a wreck before.

Wentworth heaved himself to his feet, plunged upward along steps that had grown steeper with the cant of the vessel. A man blundered into him. Wentworth raked out his left hand like a claw, caught a lifebelt that was solid and laced tightly to a man's body. He fired point-blank. The man's breath wheezed out.

Without a pause, Wentworth raced on. His jaw was grimly set. If he found anyone else in a dependable life belt, that man would die also. It would mean he was one of the murdering crew.

"Boats and lifebelts are no good!" he shouted as he ran. "Boats and lifebelts are no good! Don't trust them. Jump to the rocks!"

From forward, a man's voice took up the cry.

Wentworth recognized the hoarse tones. It was the officer who had been on the bridge. A man's hand seized Wentworth's arm.

"The sailor says the belts are all right," the man whimpered. "See, it's holding him up!"

"Where?" asked Wentworth.

He made out the sailor as the man pointed, a head that rose and fell on the water. Deliberately he raised his automatic and fired.

"Good God!" the man screeched beside him.

"You killed him."

"Certainly," Wentworth said. "This boat was wrecked on

purpose. The crew are murderers, the same ones who sank the other boats. Any man in a lifebelt that works is a murderer."

"Do you mean it?" the man gasped "Who are you?"

"The police," snapped Wentworth. "Do you want a gun?"

For a moment the man was silent while panic swirled past, then he cursed roughly. "Do I want a gun? I'll kill every damned sailor I see!"

Wentworth gave the man two guns and ammunition. "If you find another man who feels the way you do, let him have the second gun," he ordered. Then he battled his way forward. He heard a scattering gun fire there, the hoarse curses of the officer.

"Mutiny, by God!" he swore. "Take that, you dog!" His pistol cracked and a man screamed.

Wentworth pushed on through the crowd. "Don't trust the belts or boats!" he cried. "Jump to the rocks!"

To his right and above him a pistol cracked.

Wentworth sent three shots to answer it and the gun did not speak again. He pushed forward.

Suddenly Kirkpatrick was at his side. "Bowfee is safe on top the table-rock with Apollo on guard," he said. "I shot three of the crew in the water and the captain seems to have most of the others holed up in upper cabin. The passengers are getting ashore... Arthur Merriwell and that girl are with them. God only knows how they got aboard."

"The young fools!" Wentworth swore, but he felt a glow within him for he knew the girl had come to help her benefactor, the Spider. "Where's old Merriwell?" he asked.

"His Negro is carrying him up to the table-rock now," Kirkpatrick replied. "It's lucky that rock is so high. This storm is going to kick up some waves."

WENTWORTH GRUNTED. "There's thirty feet clear above high water level, and the reef will help break the waves. I think it will be safe enough. Let's help the captain collar those sailors, then get up on the rock ourselves. Bowfee might work up sympathy among that crowd and get loose."

"With Apollo on guard?" Kirkpatrick was savagely amused.

Wentworth's lips parted in a hard-lipped smile; picturing the huge Great Dane on guard beside the helpless publisher.

"Agreed," he said, "but a bullet could stop Apollo, and there must be some guns in the crowd."

They hurried to the captain's side. "I've got about seven men up in that cabin," he told them. "But I can't make them surrender even by threatening to blow up the boat. It'll be dark soon. After that we won't stand much chance of holding them."

"The best move," Wentworth said slowly, "is for all of us to get up on top that table-rock and try to summon help by signals of some kind. If I'm not mistaken more killers will come by other boats."

The captain cursed. "My rockets are up there where those men are," he rasped. "How the hell can I signal anybody?"

Wentworth shrugged. "I still think we ought to get up on the rock. The reason these men won't surrender is that they're expecting help. It stands to reason the gang behind this would send out other boats...."

He broke off as the muffled chugging of a powerful launch drifted down the night air. The wind was rising, moaning around the listed decks and the clouds had blotted out the last ray of light. The captain smashed a flurry of shots into the cabin where the men crouched; defiant yells answered. He cupped his hands whooped toward the sound of the motor, asking help.

"You fool," said Wentworth dispassionately.

"Now, we have no choice but to retreat. That boat carries killers. I wanted to take them by surprise, but you've spoiled that."

The captain cursed with chagrin. "Reckon you're right," he said. "Let's go."

"You two go ahead," Wentworth ordered. "I have one more little thing to do."

Kirkpatrick and the captain sprang to the rocks under the cover of the deepening darkness and Wentworth delayed to spill oil from a half-dozen emergency lanterns upon the heaped up furniture of a *salon*. Against the background of the fire pile he placed a lighted lantern, then he, too, clambered to the rocks. The glimmer of the lantern was faintly visible through an opened door.

SLOWLY HE made his way over the slippery reef against which the seas were beginning to thunder softly, sucking back with a slobbering moan among the upthrust fangs. Kirkpatrick and the captain met him at the brow of the table-rock, reached by a steep and twisting climb.

"Let's get wood together for a beacon," Wentworth panted, hardly waiting to reach the crest before he spoke.

"We thought of that," Kirkpatrick raised his voice above the piping of the wind. "But if we lighted it, we would be easy targets for men on the boat."

As he spoke a blue-white finger of light swept at the rocks from the east and instantly a spurting dance of powder flame began on the top deck of the wrecked steamer. Bullets whistled past. Men shouted and flung themselves flat on the rock top, but actually there was little danger. The searchlight of the motor-boat rose at a sharp angle, slanting upward past the edge of the rock-table but exposing none of its top surface.

"You see," said Kirkpatrick, "lighting a fire would be signing our death warrant."

Wentworth nodded. "Still, I think the fire should be laid, ready to touch off at a moment's notice. If we stay here until morning without help reaching us—and I see small chance of anyone getting to us before then since we weren't expected back until late tomorrow—we'll be just as good targets as we would be in the fire light. We'll wait a while after we lay it, but if no help comes, we'd better light it."

He walked slowly to the windward side of the rock while men went about the task of laying the fire on the shoreward side away from the wreck. When he had reached the verge, he turned to face the fifty-odd men who crouched atop the rock.

"Men!" he shouted, and the wind carried his voice strongly to them all. "Men! We're safe here as long as that path up the rocks is watched, no matter how many men they bring against us. We'll just sit tight until morning."

Kirkpatrick had caught up with him now and they stood together, talking softly. "I've got an idea for trapping Boise if he's guilty," Wentworth said. "I've just announced that the path is the key to the capture of the rock. I'll take care that Boise knows about the fire being laid. Then we'll watch him. If he makes a move to knock over the guard on the path, or to light the fire, we'll know he's guilty—and we can find out more about that shoulder wound of his.

"That sounds workable," Kirkpatrick agreed, "but we want to be prepared to smash any attack that results. One of us will have to watch the beacon and one the path, while another man is posted conspicuously at both places."

Wentworth nodded. "You're right. If there's any slip up in either place, it won't make any difference if we do discover Boise is guilty. They'll wipe us out in no time."

"I'll watch the beacon," Kirkpatrick said, "and you—"

"Put your hands up, both of you," a man said quietly. Wentworth whirled and a flashlight struck blindingly into his eyes.

"Or don't put your hands up, if you like," broke in the deep growl of Bowfee. "I'd enjoy putting a bullet through both of you."

Wentworth's lips were tight against his teeth.

He knew that first quiet voice, too. It was Boise, the man he suspected of being the false Spider. But it would do no good to grab for a gun in the face of their leveled weapons. These two would like nothing better than an opportunity to shoot them both down.

"That's sensible," Bowfee growled, as Wentworth lifted his hands.

"Tie them up, Bowfee," Boise said calmly. "I can see now that you were right. This man with Kirkpatrick, this professor, is actually Richard Wentworth, the Spider!"

He stepped close and seized Wentworth's wig, ripped it free.

"The Spider!" Boise jeered. "I knew I'd catch you in the end!"

"**BETTER PUT** out that light," said Wentworth quietly, "or you'll have us all killed."

As if that had been a signal, a ragged volley of shots cut across the wind from the stranded steamer.

"Lie down on the ground," Boise ordered, holding the light on them despite a sporadic hail of lead, until both Wentworth and Kirkpatrick had been bound hand and foot. Bowfee was vicious in his tying, jerking the ropes deep into the flesh. Passengers who had fled the boat began to gather about then and a few asked timid questions. Merriwell came up, borne in the arms of his Negro servant.

"What's the meaning of this?" he asked sharply. Boise glanced at him, then back at the prisoners and finally snapped off the light.

"The meaning is," said Boise, "that this man who came aboard as a professor is the Spider! The other man is his accomplice!"

Merriwell's protest was drowned in a rising murmur from the crowd.

"The Spider!" a man shouted. "The Spider!"

"He wrecked the boat!" another cried. "He burned a tenement!"

"He murdered Robert Kenton!"

The litany of the crimes of the false Spider rose angrily into the howling of the storm. It pierced even the louder thunder of the waves. Lightning flashed across the close-crowding clouds and Kirkpatrick cursed under his breath.

"Boise," he called. "If you don't do something quick, that mob is going to kill us!"

"Serve you right," snarled Bowfee. "I'll lend a hand myself."

"There'll be no lynch law here," Boise snapped. Wentworth lay supine upon the ground, stared at the cloudrack that scudded thickly past. He had heard before this the roar of a mob, thirsting for his blood, accusing him of crimes that his enemies had committed. But never before had his own position seemed so hopeless. Bound hand and foot, he lay in a place from which there was no escape, while the very people he had sought to save were baying for his death.

Even so, his thoughts were for the good of those people. In this mad mob spirit, there was no one to guard the head of the path, no one to see that the beacon was not lighted.

"Boise!" he shouted, raising his voice above the mob roar. "Boise! Guard the path! Guard the beacon!"

Boise was confronting the crowd, his back to Wentworth and Kirkpatrick, a gun in his hand. He squeezed light from his hand-torch and spattered it in the faces of the men.

"There'll be no lynch law," Boise shouted, his quiet voice raised for once. "I'll shoot the first man who moves to harm my prisoners!"

The gun spat red fire above the crowds. "Get back!" he ordered.

"Boise!" Wentworth shouted. "For God's sake, watch the path and the beacon!"

Boise finally caught the cry and seized upon it to help break up the mob.

"You," he stabbed light at a man, "watch the head of the path to keep anybody from coming up. You,"—the light picked out another—"get over by that pile of firewood and see nobody lights it until we're ready."

For a moment, the crowd stood sullen. The two men did not move to obey. Boise leveled his pistol. "You march for the head of the path," he snapped, "before I count three, or I'll shoot you down. *One—*"

Wentworth ceased his shout. If Boise were the false Spider, he was doing the real Spider a damned good turn just now.

"*Two!*" Boise said.

If they didn't hurry, there would be no use in guarding the path. There had been no shots from the steamer for minutes now. Probably the killers were on their way to scale the path, having discovered the preoccupation of the crowd.

Boise raised his pistol an inch to bring it in line with the man's head.

"*Three!*" he said.

The man jerked into motion, and with him, the mob began to move restlessly. Suddenly a flickering glow rose on the far side of the rock, a red growing brightness in the air.

"The beacon! The beacon!" Wentworth shouted. Two shots rang out sharply through the night. "Freeze, all of you!" a man shouted. "A machine gun's trained on you."

A BRIEF flurry of shots jabbered from the machine gun. Frightened shouts flew to the heavens. The leaping flames of the beacon showed the panicked, milling of the men, showed a solid line of guns trained on them by gangsters from the steamer.

From among the killers' close ranks slipped a cloaked, hunch-backed figure with a broad-brimmed hat drawn down over its eyes. He shuffled forward toward the prisoners, head turning from side to side as he studied the faces revealed in the increasing glare of firelight, faces pasty white despite the roseate glow.

Kirkpatrick cursed low in amazement. "Dick," he gasped out. "Dick, there… there's the Spider!"

Wentworth smiled slightly. "Merriwell here?" he asked.

"Yes, I'm here," the millionaire snapped. "You've got a better chance of surviving than anyone else, I think," Wentworth said. "They could hold you for ransom. If you get back to the city, will you see to it that this is known?"

"This Spider business? Yes, but I won't get back," Merriwell snarled.

"Bowfee? Boise?" Wentworth raised his voice. "Yes," both agreed from a little distance.

Wentworth frowned. He had been wrong then in suspecting Boise of being the false Spider. The hunch-backed figure was moving closer now to the ranks of captive men and they shrank back as he advanced, all save Wentworth and Kirkpatrick.

The man came on until he stood over Wentworth, who squinted his eyes in a vain effort to make out the man's face.

"Ah, Wentworth," the man said suavely. "You made a certain boast a while ago that you had evidence which would prove me guilty of a large number of crimes. You see, I have spies even in Phineas Merriwell's house."

"You are a murderer," Wentworth said clearly, strongly. "A murderer of the innocent. You tortured Robert Kenton to death, set fire to tenements, helped crucify those people. And you are not the real Spider. He would not do such things."

The false Spider chuckled. "So what?" he jeered.

"You have evidence to convict me, you say, if you live. If you die, you can't prove it."

His hand whisked from beneath the long black robe that swayed from his hunched back, that flapped like evil wings in the wind. A short sword glittered in his hand. He presented its point at Wentworth's throat. "You'll never prove it, Wentworth."

He drew back his hand to thrust the blade through Wentworth's throat.

CHAPTER 12
WHEN HOPE IS GONE

WITH THAT sword poised, with his eyes glaring down into the eyes of his helpless captive, the false Spider paused. He chuckled.

"No, no, not yet!" he muttered. "We must wait a while. Wait until you see how you have failed, how we will reign when you are dead."

He whirled toward the men with the guns.

"Line them up!" he shouted.

A deep curse rose in Wentworth's throat. He was to be spared for a few seconds, but at the cost of these fifty other human lives. He tossed his body on the earth, rolled his head, and abruptly, he stiffened. Two things gave him hope, a glimpse of a girl's red dress, and a sound back in the midst of the crowd. Back there he had heard a man yip out excitedly, and he had heard a growl.

Good Lord, was it possible! Wentworth puckered his lips and emitted a low weird whistle. Then he cocked his ear to listen. The leaping flames of the beacon already were dying and shadows were crouching over the crowd. In a few minutes darkness would settle again over the doomed men—but not many moments were needed to wipe out these fifty with a machine gun.

Once more, with dying hope, Wentworth puckered his lips in a whistle, then he peered about. In the front ranks of the crowd, not fifteen feet away, Bowfee stood. Boise was with him, but Merriwell was not in sight.

"Bowfee!" Wentworth cried. "Bowfee! It's the double cross! When that machine gun talks, it will pronounce the death sentence on you, too. Don't you see it, Bowfee?"

He was watching the hunch-backed figure of the false Spider hurry toward the machine gunner. Anything Wentworth *was* to do would have to be done swiftly. He jerked his head toward Bowfee.

"What are you talking about?" the publisher growled.

"Don't you know the answer, Bowfee?"

Wentworth jeered. "The answer is: *Where is Merriwell?*"

A startled curse ripped out through the encroaching darkness.

"Merriwell!" Bowfee shouted. "Merriwell, where are you?"

Bowfee took three blundering paces forward of the ranks of the crowd and peered about him. Wentworth's heart gave a great bound within him. The killers were all looking at Bowfee now, as was the crowd about him, and with straining ears, Wentworth caught a sound he had scarcely dared hope to hear even after that growl had startled men in the midst of the crowd. He heard the soft padding of animal feet, the snuffing of a dog that sought a scent, then Apollo, great Apollo, was beside him in the darkness!

Something like a sob rose in Wentworth's throat. He had not dared hope that the dog was alive. When he had seen Bowfee free, Boise beside him, he had been confident that his great dog was dead. But that growl had led him to the guess that Apollo had only been knocked out and had that moment regained consciousness.

"Charge, Apollo!" Wentworth whispered.

"Charge!"

With a low fierce snarl, the dog shot out across the short distance that separated him from the killers. Frightened shouts flung from the men, a spattering of gunfire. Wentworth was sure that he had sent the dog to his death, but it was the only chance. He must create a diversion if he were to escape and save these men and the city from disaster.

"Arthur!" he whispered softly. "Caroline! Cut my ropes now."

As he saw the girl crouch and crawl on her hands and knees to him, he shouted again to Bowfee.

"Don't you see what Merriwell's disappearance means, Bowfee?" he cried. "First, he tried to keep from coming on the trip. Then when you made him come, he skipped out so you would be killed by the machine gunner."

THE FALSE Spider had reached his men now, and whirled with the machine gun gripped in his hands. Its muzzle sought

Apollo, but the dog was bounding among the killers like an avenging demon. Men screamed and fired at him. Wentworth saw Apollo go down, roll and vanish into the shadows behind the men. He bit his lips to choke down his grief. This time, surely, Apollo was dead.

He swept the ranks of the killers while the girl slashed his bonds. Suddenly, without warning, Merriwell appeared in the forefront of the killers, carried easily in the arms of the giant black. His voice lifted in cracked laughter, the crazy, eerie laughter that had marked all the Torture Kills.

"You called me, Bowfee," he jeered. "I come to pronounce death on you. You're getting too ambitious."

A gun flamed in Bowfee's fist, but its blast was swallowed in the stammering burst of the false Spider's gun. Bowfee wilted, pitching forward, but his one shot had found its mark. Merriwell was cursing shrilly and Wentworth saw him and his Negro tumble to the rock. The false Spider handed the machine gun to a gangster, ran to the fallen leader—and Wentworth's hands came free.

"Free Kirkpatrick, Caroline," he said swiftly, and twin guns leaped to his hands from armpit holsters. But eager as he was for the fray, he stayed his hand. The gangsters seemed stunned by the death of two leaders. Wentworth drew a bead on the machine gunner and *waited*. Abruptly, Kirkpatrick was at his side.

"On the steamer," Wentworth said rapidly. "An oil lantern burning. Shoot the glass out of it and you'll set the steamer afire."

"But why?"

"It will put the light behind these killers, give us a target!" Wentworth told him. "Also it will signal a boat load of private detectives I hired to shoot hell out of this bunch!"

Kirkpatrick growled, "That's swell," and dodged off into the darkness. Wentworth lifted his automatic, searching for the false Spider. The man had vanished!

With a cry of anger, Wentworth scrambled to his feet, poured lead into the ranks of the killers, dropping the machine gunner first. A sharp crackle of return fire ripped out from the gang ranks. Behind Wentworth, men screamed. A man sprang to his side, flung down on his knee and began to shoot. It was Boise.

"Nice work," said Boise.

Wentworth did not answer. He was shooting, shooting.

Abruptly, flame licked up behind the men on the edge of the rock. Kirkpatrick's shot had found its goal. Fire was coursing over the wreck of the steamer. Wentworth's mouth twisted in a grim smile. It would serve another purpose, too. The motor-boats lay there. Not one of these criminals would escape! With swift fingers, Wentworth expelled a clip from his automatic and stuffed in a full one, jacked a shell into the chamber. A blast of gunfire in the distance told of the entrance into the battle of Wentworth's detectives.

"They're driven back some now," Wentworth said punctuating his words with lead. "If you could reach that machine gun...."

Boise snapped, "Right!" and was gone. In moments, the machine gun began to stammer.

Soon the flames leaped clear above the edge of the rock, and not a figure showed against their red and orange dance. Wentworth sprang to his feet, spun toward Merriwell and Bowfee. Both were dead. The giant Negro was sprawled beside them. Bowfee's bullet had crashed through Merriwell's throat and buried itself in the giant's chest. There were only these three dead. The rest had fled.

For a brief instant, Wentworth paused and pressed something that glittered to the forehead of each corpse. Then he raced on across the stretch where the dead lay thick-piled, reached the brink of the path and half-fell, half-climbed down its steep way. SOMEWHERE OUT here, the false Spider had fled. Abruptly, Wentworth checked, staring at the flames of the wrecked steamer. On its upper deck capered a cloaked hunchbacked figure—the man he sought. Wentworth strained his dim eyes, then he understood. What had at first seemed to be a fantastic death dance became clear. The man was moving along an invisible rope that stretched past the flaming part of the ship to its rear structure where the sleek nose of a speedboat glinted. The false Spider crept hand over hand, swaying in the wind, and he seemed to use his left arm with great difficulty.

The black fangs of rocks reached up for him from below, frothing with the sloshing foam of the mounting waves. Wentworth realized that the man must be using some such wisp of silk as he himself employed. The man had certainly gone in for his imitation in every detail, but he would be a fool to trust his life to that silken line.

Wentworth's ropes were made of the highest quality silk and he tested them at least once a week for the swift weakening that attacks such fibers. That man would know nothing of such precautions.

A shout arose in Wentworth's throat. As if in interpretation of his thoughts, the caped flapping figure plunged downward and his shriek sang back across the wind. Then he dropped to the pointed fangs of the rocks and the tide sucked and lapped about him. Except for the wash of the water, he did not move. Wentworth saw then that Kirkpatrick stood out against the flames, far down toward the point where the steamer had been stranded.

Kirkpatrick had been ready to shoot at the fleeing killer, but, like Wentworth, he had held his hand to watch his struggle. Now he turned back toward the rock and came at a swift jig. Wentworth turned away, found Apollo and bent above the great body. Joy thrilled through him, for though bullets had laid him low, it did not seem to Wentworth that he was gravely wounded. He jerked to his feet and became aware that Boise was standing beside him. He turned, and the man's hand reached out for his.

"Wentworth," Boise said, "I want you to accept my apologies for accusing you. I'd like to apologize to the Spider, too, for confusing him with this murderer here tonight. At any rate, I'll see the newspapers get the right of that."

"Quite all right," Wentworth said. "However, if you feel that any restitution is due...."

"I do! I do!" Boise cried.

Wentworth smiled slightly. "Then, why not resign and ask the Mayor to reinstate Kirkpatrick? He only helped me because he knew I was being framed."

Boise stared at Wentworth for a minute, then his head nodded slowly twice.

"That, I think, would be an excellent idea," he said.

Kirkpatrick came panting up the path. "It was Jack Hayes," he gasped. "I could see his face as he lay there in the water. He must have stabbed Boise just to turn suspicion on him."

Wentworth nodded slowly, told Kirkpatrick what Boise had decided. Kirkpatrick flashed one of his rare smiles.

"I want you for an assistant," he said. "That was splendid work you did, stopping that mob."

Boise smiled quietly. "The man who really should head the police," he said, "is this gentleman here, Mr. Wentworth. How in the world did you ever figure out this line-up of crooks?"

"I suspected Merriwell first when I learned that his adopted son was engaged to Caroline Davis," he said, "the girl whose grandfather was accused of those crucifixions. Not one of Merriwell's adopted children has married. I found that out after I heard of the engagement. Yet they are nice kids, with plenty of money back of them. It was suspicious, that was all. A hunch, if you like. I had always wondered why Preston Davis was selected for the rap in that series of murders, I believe it was partly to keep Arthur from marrying Caroline."

WENTWORTH SHRUGGED, smiling slightly. "I'll concede that was no basis for suspecting a man," he continued, "But when I went to Merriwell for help against these criminals, I found he had profited enormously by everything that had been done by them. Apparently he was helping out companies, driven close to bankruptcy by the Murder Trust's depredations, by the

tenement fires and murder of officials, by the sabotage of ships—
By the way, that first ship of Merriwell's that sank was owned by
a separate small line unconnected with his many other excursion
ships. That has been the only mishap to one of his ships, and he
was advertising the safety of these other lines of his. That's how
he was cashing in on the sinking of other boats. He would have
bought out his rivals in the end, I think.

"I planned this trap on board the ship for Merriwell and
Bowfee. I still was not sure of Merriwell's guilt. It seemed fantastic to suspect him. Such a great philanthropist! A gentle man
who was gypped by his own lawyer! Hell, I think he fired the
shot that killed Cartwright.

"I gave him a chance to wriggle out of coming on the trip
today and he jumped at it—but Bowfee was too clever to allow
him to do that. Bowfee had been growing in power and figured
that Merriwell planned his death, or else he plotted to kill
Merriwell himself on this trip today. Bowfee was a big frog in
the puddle, and probably figured himself a little bigger even
than Merriwell."

Footsteps near turned their attention to two approaching
figures. Young Arthur Merriwell, the girl, Caroline Davis at
his side, walked slowly forward. Arthur's face was haggard with
pain.

"I still find all this hard to believe," he said, "but I want to
promise that whatever money of—of father's I can obtain will
be spent righting the wrongs he has done. Caroline's grandfather will be freed now, of course…" He turned to her and the
girl smiled gently up at him.

"Hey!" a shrill cry rang out behind them. "Hey!" A man came pounding across the table rock, his arms flung high. "Hey!" he screamed. "The Spider! The Spider!"

Boise cursed, deep in his throat, whirled about with his automatic in hand.

The man pounded up, clutched at Boise and stood pointing back.

"What is it, you fool!" Boise demanded.

"Over there," the man panted. "The Spider!—"

"The Spider what?" Boise was frantic.

"The Spider put his seal on those two dead men, on Bowfee and Merriwell," the man got out with a gulp. "It's on their foreheads, a red Spider with hairy legs and fangs and—"

Boise cursed, raced across the table-rock toward where the bodies sprawled. Wentworth stood, staring at the burning ship and Kirkpatrick looked at him.

"You killed those men, Dick," said Kirkpatrick.

"Indirectly, of course. Still the credit is yours. It is not like the Spider to take credit from another this way."

Wentworth smiled slowly. "Perhaps," he said, "the Spider is jealous of my triumph."

Kirkpatrick continued to stare at him and slowly, he, too, began to whistle and both men's smiles were grim.

"Perhaps…" he agreed softly.

POPULAR HERO PULPS AVAILABLE NOW:

THE SPIDER
- ❏ #1: The Spider Strikes — $13.95
- ❏ #2: The Wheel of Death — $13.95
- ❏ #3: Wings of the Black Death — $13.95
- ❏ #4: City of Flaming Shadows — $13.95
- ❏ #5: Empire of Doom! — $13.95
- ❏ #6: Citadel of Hell — $13.95
- ❏ #7: The Serpent of Destruction — $13.95
- ❏ #8: The Mad Horde — $13.95
- ❏ #9: Satan's Death Blast — $13.95
- ❏ #10: The Corpse Cargo — $13.95
- ❏ #11: Prince of the Red Looters — $13.95
- ❏ #12: Reign of the Silver Terror — $13.95
- ❏ #13: Builders of the Dark Empire — $13.95
- ❏ *NEW:* #14: Death's Crimson Juggernaut — $13.95

OPERATOR 5
- ❏ #1: The Masked Invasion — $13.95
- ❏ #2: The Invisible Empire — $13.95
- ❏ #3: The Yellow Scourge — $13.95
- ❏ #4: The Melting Death — $13.95
- ❏ #5: Cavern of the Damned — $13.95
- ❏ #6: Master of Broken Men — $13.95
- ❏ #7: Invasion of the Dark Legions — $13.95

THE MYSTERIOUS WU FANG
- ❏ #1: The Case of the Six Coffins — $12.95
- ❏ #2: The Case of the Scarlet Feather — $12.95
- ❏ #3: The Case of the Yellow Mask — $12.95
- ❏ #4: The Case of the Suicide Tomb — $12.95
- ❏ #5: The Case of the Green Death — $12.95
- ❏ #6: The Case of the Black Lotus — $12.95
- ❏ #7: The Case of the Hidden Scourge — $12.95

G-8 AND HIS BATTLE ACES
- ❏ #1: The Bat Staffel — $13.95

CAPTAIN SATAN
- ❏ #1: The Mask of the Damned — $13.95
- ❏ #2: Parole for the Dead — $13.95
- ❏ #3: The Dead Man Express — $13.95
- ❏ *NEW:* #4: A Ghost Rides the Dawn — $13.95

DUSTY AYRES AND HIS BATTLE BIRDS
- ❏ #1: Black Lightning! — $13.95
- ❏ #2: Crimson Doom — $13.95
- ❏ #3: The Purple Tornado — $13.95
- ❏ #4: The Screaming Eye — $13.95
- ❏ #5: The Green Thunderbolt — $13.95
- ❏ #6: The Red Destroyer — $13.95
- ❏ #7: The White Death — $13.95
- ❏ #8: The Black Avenger — $13.95
- ❏ #9: The Silver Typhoon — $13.95
- ❏ #10: The Troposphere F-S — $13.95
- ❏ #11: The Blue Cyclone — $13.95
- ❏ #12: The Tesla Raiders — $13.95

DR. YEN SIN
- ❏ #1: Mystery of the Dragon's Shadow — $12.95
- ❏ #2: Mystery of the Golden Skull — $12.95
- ❏ #3: Mystery of the Singing Mummies — $12.95

MAVERICKS
- ❏ #1: Five Against the Law — $12.95
- ❏ #2: Mesquite Manhunters — $12.95
- ❏ #3: Bait for the Lobo Pack — $12.95
- ❏ #4: Doc Grimson's Outlaw Posse — $12.95
- ❏ #5: Charlie Parr's Gunsmoke Cure — $12.95